CHILDREN'S
CLASSICS

ROBINSON CRUSOE

Daniel Defoe

D1409030

Bloomsbury Books
London

This edition published 1994 by Bloomsbury Books, an
imprint of The Godfrey Cave Group, 42 Bloomsbury Street,
London, WC1B 3QJ.

ISBN 1 85471 280 2

Printed and bound by Firmin-Didot (France),
Group Herissey. No d'impression : 26463.

ROBINSON CRUSOE

Robinson Crusoe

We set out from the Brazils for the Guinea coast on the 1st day of September, 1659, I being supercargo to manage the trade upon the coast of Guinea. Our ship was about 120 tons burthen; carried six guns and fourteen men, besides the master, his boy, and myself. We had on board no large cargo of goods, except of such toys as were fit for our trade with the negroes—such as beads, bits of glass, shells and odd trifles, especially little looking-glasses, knives, scissors, hatchets, and the like.

We passed the line in about twelve days' time; and were by our last observation in 7 degrees 22 minutes northern latitude, when a violent tornado or hurricane took us quite out of our knowledge. It began from the south-east, came about to the north-west and then settled into the north-east; from whence it blew in such a terrible manner that for twelve days together we could do nothing but drive, and, scudding away before it, let it carry us whither ever fate and the fury of the winds directed. And during these twelve days I need not say that I expected every day to be swallowed up; nor, indeed, did any in the ship expect to save their lives.

In this distress, the wind still blowing very hard, one of our men early in the morning cried out "Land!" and we had no sooner run out of the cabin to look out in hopes of seeing whereabouts in the world we were, but the ship struck upon a sand, and in a moment, her motion being so stopped, the sea broke over her in such a manner, that we expected we should all have perished immediately, and we were immediately driven into our close quarters to shelter us from the very foam and spray of the sea. We sat looking one upon another, and expecting death every moment, and every man acting accordingly as preparing for another world, for there was little or nothing more for us to do in this. That which was our present comfort, and all the comfort we had, was that, contrary to our expectation, the ship did not break yet, and that the master said the wind began to abate.

Now, though we thought that the wind did a little abate, yet the ship having thus struck upon the sand, and sticking too fast for us to expect her getting off, we were in a dreadful condition indeed, and had nothing to do but to think of saving our lives as well as we could.

In this distress the mate of our vessel lays hold of the boat, and with the help of the rest of the men they got her slung over the ship's side, and getting all into her, let go, and committed ourselves, being

eleven in number, to God's mercy and the wild sea:
for though the storm was abated considerably, yet
the sea went dreadfully high upon the shore.

And now our case was very dismal indeed; for we
all saw plainly that the sea went so high that the boat
could not live, and that we should be inevitably
drowned. As to making sail, we had none; nor, if we
had, could we have done anything with it: so we
worked at the oar towards the land, though with heavy
hearts, like men going to execution; for we all knew
that when the boat came nearer the shore she would
be dashed in a thousand pieces by the breach of the
sea. However, we committed our souls to God in the
most earnest manner, and the wind driving us towards the shore we hastened our destruction with
our own hands, pulling as well as we could towards
land.

What the shore was—whether rock or sand, whether
steep or shoal—we knew not; the only hope that
could rationally give us the least shadow of expectation was, if we might happen into some bay or gulf,
or the mouth of some river, where by great chance
we might have run our boat in, or got under the lee
of the land, and perhaps made smooth water. But
there was nothing of this appeared; but as we made
nearer and nearer the shore, the land looked more
frightful than the sea.

After we had rowed or rather driven about a league

and a half, as we reckoned it, a raging wave, moun-
tain-like, came rolling astern of us, and plainly bade
us expect the *coup-de-grace*. In a word, it took us
with such a fury, that it overset the boat at once,
and, separating us as well from the boat as from one
another, gave us not time hardly to say, O God! for
we were all swallowed up in a moment.

Nothing can describe the confusion of thought
which I felt when I sunk into the water; for though I
swam very well, yet I could not deliver myself from
the waves so as to draw breath, till that a wave,
having driven me or rather carried me a vast way on
towards the shore, and having spent itself, went back,
and left me upon the land almost dry, but half-dead
with the water I took in. I had so much presence of
mind as well as breath left that, seeing myself nearer
the mainland than I expected, I got upon my feet,
and endeavoured to make on towards the land as fast
as I could before another wave should return and
take me up again. But I soon found it was impossible to avoid it; for I saw the sea come after me as
high as a great hill, and as furious as an enemy
which I had no means or strength to contend with.
My business was to hold my breath and rise myself
upon the water if I could, and so by swimming to
preserve my breathing and pilot myself towards the
shore if possible; my greatest concern now being
that the sea, as it would carry me a great way to-

wards the shore when it came on, might not carry me back again with it when it gave back towards the sea.

The wave that came upon me again buried me at once twenty or thirty feet deep in its own body; and I could feel myself carried with a mighty force and swiftness towards the shore a very great way; but I held my breath, and assisted myself to swim still forward with all my might. I was ready to burst with holding my breath, when, as I felt myself rising up, so to my immediate relief I found my head and hands shoot out above the surface of the water; and though it was not two seconds of time that I could keep myself so, yet it relieved me greatly, gave me breath and new courage. I was covered again with water a good while, but not so long but I held it out; and finding the water had spent itself and began to return, I struck forward against the return of the waves, and felt ground again with my feet. I stood still a few moments to recover breath, and till the water went from me, and then took to my heels and ran with what strength I had farther towards the shore. But neither would this deliver me from the fury of the sea, which came pouring in after me again, and twice more I was lifted up by the waves and carried forwards as before, the shore being very flat.

The last time of these two had well near been fatal to me; for the sea, having hurried me along as be-

fore, landed me, or rather dashed me against a piece
of rock, and that with such force, as it left me sense-
less, and indeed helpless as to my own deliverance:
for the blow taking my side and breast, beat the
breath as it were quite out of my body, and had it
returned again immediately, I must have been stran-
gled in the water; but I recovered a little before the
return of the waves, and seeing I should be covered
again with the water, I resolved to hold fast by a
piece of the rock, and so to hold my breath, if possible, till the wave went back. Now as the waves were
not so high as at first, being near land, I held my
hold till the wave abated, and then fetched another
run, which brought me so near the shore, that the
next wave though it went over me, yet did not so
swallow me up as to carry me away; and the next
run I took I got to the mainland, where, to my great
comfort, I clambered up the cliffs of the shore and
sat me down upon the grass, free from danger, and
quite out of the reach of the water.

I was now landed, and safe on shore, and began to
look up and thank God that my life was saved in a
case wherein there was some minutes before scarce
any room to hope. I walked about on the shore lift-
ing up my hands, and my whole being, as I may say,
wrapped up in the contemplation of my deliverance,
making a thousand gestures and motions which I
cannot describe, reflecting upon all my comrades

that were drowned, and that there should not be one soul saved but myself; for, as for them, I never saw them afterwards, or any sign of them, except three of their hats, one cap, and two shoes that were not fellows.

I cast my eyes to the stranded vessel, when the breach and froth of the sea being so big, I could hardly see it, it lay so far off, and considered, "Lord, how was it possible I could get on shore?"

After I had solaced my mind with the comfortable part of my condition, I began to look round me to see what kind of place I was in, and what was next to be done, and I soon found my comforts abate, and that, in a word, I had a dreadful deliverance; for I was wet, had no clothes to shift me, nor anything either to eat or drink to comfort me, neither did I see any prospect before me but that of perishing with hunger, or being devoured by wild beasts. And that which was particularly afflicting to me was, that I had no weapon either to hunt and kill any creature for my sustenance, or to defend myself against any other creature that might desire to kill me for theirs; in a word, I had nothing about me but a knife, a tobacco-pipe, and a little tobacco in a box. This was all my provision, and this threw me into terrible agonies of mind, and for a while I ran about like a madman. Night coming upon me, I began, with a heavy heart, to consider what would be my lot if there were any ravenous beasts in that country, seeing at night they always come abroad for their prey.

All the remedy that offered to my thoughts at that time was, to get up into a thick bushy tree like a fir, but thorny, which grew near me, and where I resolved to sit all night, and consider the next day what death I should die; for as yet I saw no prospect of life. I walked about a furlong from the shore to see if I could find any fresh water to drink, which I did, to my great joy; and having drunk, and put a little tobacco in my mouth to prevent hunger, I went to the tree, and getting up into it, endeavoured to place myself so as that if I should sleep I might not fall; and having cut me a short stick like a truncheon for my defence, I took up my lodging, and having been excessively fatigued, I fell fast asleep, and slept as comfortably as, I believe, few could have done in my condition, and found myself the most refreshed with it that I think I ever was on such an occasion.

When I waked it was broad day, the weather clear, and the storm abated, so that the sea did not rage and swell as before; but that which surprised me most was, that the ship was lifted off in the night from the sand where she lay by the swelling of the tide, and was driven up almost as far as the rock which I first mentioned, where I had been so bruised by the dashing me against it; this being within about a mile from the shore where I was, and the ship seeming to stand upright still, I wished myself on board, that at least I might have some necessary things for my use.

When I came down from my apartment in the tree, I looked about me again, and the first thing I found was the boat, which lay as the wind and the sea had tossed her up upon the land, about two miles on my right hand. I walked as far as I could upon the shore to have got to her, but found a neck or inlet of water between me and the boat which was about half a mile broad; so I came back for the present, being more intent upon getting at the ship, where I hoped to find something for my present subsistence.

A little after noon I found the sea very calm and the tide ebbed so far out that I could come within a quarter of a mile of the ship. And here I found a fresh renewing of my grief; for I saw evidently that if we had kept on board we had been all safe—that is to say, we had all got safe on shore, and I had not been so miserable as to be left entirely destitute of all comfort and company as I now was. This forced tears from my eyes again, but as there was little relief in that, I resolved, if possible, to get to the ship; so I pulled off my clothes, for the weather was hot to extremity, and took the water. But when I came to the ship, my difficulty was still greater to know how to get on board; for as she lay aground and high out of the water, there was nothing within my reach to lay hold of. I swam round her twice, and the second time I spied a small piece of a rope, which I wondered I did not see at first, hang down by the fore-chains so low as that with great difficulty I got hold of it, and by the help of that rope got up into the forecastle of the ship. Here I found that the ship was bulged,* and had a great deal of water in her hold, but that she lay so on the side of a bank of hard sand, or rather earth, and her stern lay lifted up upon the bank, and her head low almost to the water. By this means all her quarter was free, and all that was in that part was dry; for you may be sure my first work was to search and to see what was spoiled and what was free. And first I found that all the ship's provisions were dry and untouched by the water, and being very well disposed to eat, I went to the bread-room and filled my pockets with biscuit, and ate it as I went about other things, for I had no time to lose. I also found some rum in the great cabin, of which I took a large dram, and which I had indeed need enough of to spirit me for what was before me. Now I wanted nothing but a boat to furnish myself with many things which I foresaw would be very necessary to me.

It was in vain to sit still and wish for what was not to be had, and this extremity roused my application. We had several spare yards, and two or three large

* Some of the timbers struck off so as to cause a leak

spars of wood, and a spare top-mast or two in the ship. I resolved to fall to work with these, and flung as many of them overboard as I could manage of their weight, tying every one with a rope that they might not drive away. When this was done, I went down the ship's side, and pulling them to me, I tied four of them fast together at both ends as well as I could, in the form of a raft, and laying two or three short pieces of plank upon them crossways, I found I could walk upon it very well, but that it was not able to bear any great weight, the pieces being too light. So I went to work, and with the carpenter's saw I cut a spare top-mast into three lengths, and added them to my raft, with a great deal of labour and pains; but hope of furnishing myself with necessaries encouraged me to go beyond what I should have been able to have done upon another occasion.

My raft was now strong enough to bear any reasonable weight. My next care was what to load it with, and how to preserve what I laid upon it from the surf of the sea. But I was not long considering this. I first laid all the planks or boards upon it that I could get, and having considered well what I most wanted, I first got three of the seamen's chests, which I had broken open and emptied, and lowered them down upon my raft. The first of these I filled with provisions—namely, bread, rice, three Dutch cheeses, five pieces of dried goat's flesh, which we lived much upon, and a little remainder of European corn which had been laid by for some fowls which we brought to sea with us; but the fowls were killed. As for liquors I found several cases of bottles belonging to our skipper, in which were some cordial waters, and in all about five or six gallons of rack.* These I stowed by themselves. While I was doing this I found the tide began to flow, though very calm, and I had the mortification to see my coat, shirt, and waistcoat, which I had left on shore upon the sand, swim away; as for my breeches, which were only linen and open-kneed, I swam on board in them and my stockings. However, this put me upon rummaging for clothes, of which I found enough, but took no more than I wanted for present use, for I had other things which my eye was more upon—as, first, tools to work with on shore, and it was after long searching that I found out the carpenter's chest, which was indeed a very useful prize to me, and much more valuable than a ship loading of gold would have been at that time. I got it down to my raft even whole as it was, without losing time to look into it, for I knew in general what it contained.

My next care was for some ammunition and arms. There were two very good fowling-pieces in the great cabin, and two pistols; these I secured first, with

* Arrack, a spirit distilled from rice or other grain, resembling gin or whisky.

some powder-horns, and a small bag of shot, and two old rusty swords. I knew there were three barrels of powder in the ship, but knew not where our gunner had stowed them; but with much search I found them, two of them dry and good, the third had taken water. Those two I got to my raft with the arms; and now I thought myself pretty well freighted, and began to think how I should get to shore with them, having neither sail, oar, nor rudder, and the least capful of wind would have overset all my navigation.

I had three encouragements—first, a smooth calm sea, second, the tide rising and setting in to the shore; third, what little wind there was blew me towards the land. And thus, having found two or three broken oars belonging to the boat, and besides the tools which were in the chest, I found two saws, an axe, and a hammer, and with this cargo I put to sea. For a mile or thereabouts my raft went very well, only that I found it drive a little distant from the place where I had landed before; by which I perceived that there was some indraught of the water, and consequently I hoped to find some creek or river there, which I might make use of as a port to get to land with my cargo.

As I imagined, so it was. There appeared before me a little opening of the land, and I found a strong current of the tide set into it; so I guided my raft as well as I could to keep in the middle of the stream. But here I had like to have suffered a second ship-wreck, which if I had, I think verily would have broken my heart; for, knowing nothing of the coast, my raft ran aground at one end of it upon a shoal, and not being aground at the other end, it wanted but a little that all my cargo had slipped off towards that end that was afloat, and so fallen into the water. I did my utmost, by setting my back against the chests, to keep them in their places, but could not thrust off the raft with all my strength, neither durst I stir from the posture I was in, but holding up the chests with all my might, stood in that manner near half an hour, in which time the rising of the water brought me a little more upon a level; and a little after, the water still rising, my raft floated again, and I thrust her off with the oar I had into the channel, and then driving up higher, I at length found myself in the mouth of a little river, with land on both sides, and a strong current or tide running up. I looked on both sides for a proper place to get to shore, for I was not willing to be driven too high up the river, hoping in time to see some ship at sea, and therefore resolve to place myself as near the coast as I could.

At length I spied a little cover on the right shore of the creek, to which with great pain and difficulty I guided my raft, and at last got so near as that, reaching ground with my oar, I could thrust her directly

in. But here I had like to have dipped all my cargo in
the sea again; for that shore lying pretty steep—that
is to say, sloping—there was no place to land. All
that I could do was to wait till the tide was at the
highest, keeping the raft with my oar like an anchor
to hold the side of it fast to the shore near a flat
piece of ground, which I expected the water would
flow over; and so it did. As soon as I found water
enough—for my raft drew about a foot of water—I
thrust her on upon that flat piece of ground, and
there fastened or moored her by sticking my two
broken oars into the ground, one on one side near
one end, and one on the other side near the other
end; and thus I lay till the water ebbed away, and
left my raft and all my cargo safe on shore.

My next work was to view the country and seek a
proper place for my habitation, and where to stow
my goods to secure them from whatever might happen. Where I was I yet knew not, whether on the
Continent or on an island, whether inhabited or not
inhabited, whether in danger of wild beasts or not.
There was a hill not above a mile from me which
rose up very steep and high, and which seemed to
overtop some other hills which lay as in a ridge
from it northward. I took out one of the fowling-
pieces and one of the pistols, and a horn of powder,
and thus armed I travelled for discovery up to the
top of that hill, where, after I had with great labour

and difficulty got to the top, I saw my fate to my great affliction—namely, that I was in an island environed every way with the sea, no land to be seen except some rocks which lay a great way off and two small islands, less than this, which lay about three leagues to the west.

I found also that the island I was in was barren, and, as I saw good reason to believe, uninhabited, except by wild beasts—of whom, however, I saw none; yet I saw abundance of fowls, but knew not their kinds, neither when I killed them could I tell what was fit for food and what not. At my coming back, I shot at a great bird which I saw sitting upon a tree on the side of a great wood. I believe it was the first gun that had been fired there since the creation of the world. I had no sooner fired, but from all the parts of the wood there arose an innumerable number of fowls of many sorts, making a confused screaming, and crying everyone according to his usual note; but not one of them of any kind that I knew. As for the creature I killed, I took it to be a kind of a hawk, its colour and beak resembling it, but had no talons or claws more than common; its flesh was carrion and fit for nothing.

Contented with this discovery, I came back to my raft, and fell to work to bring my cargo on shore, which took me up the rest of the day. And what to do with myself at night I knew not, nor indeed where to rest; for I was afraid to lie down on the ground, not knowing but some wild beast might devour me, though, as I afterwards found, there was really no need for those fears.

However, as well as I could, I barricaded myself round with the chests and boards that I had brought on shore, and made a kind of hut for that night's lodging. As for food, I yet saw not which way to supply myself, except that I had seen two or three creatures like hares run out of the wood where I shot the fowl.

I now began to consider that I might yet get a great many things out of the ship which would be useful to me, and particularly some of the rigging and sails, and such other things as might come to land; and I resolved to make another voyage on board the vessel, if possible; and as I knew that the first storm that blew must necessarily break her all in pieces, I resolved to set all other things apart, till I got everything out of the ship that I could get. Then I called a council—that is to say, in my thoughts— whether I should take back the raft; but this appeared impracticable. So I resolved to go as before, when the tide was down; and I did so, only that I stripped before I went from my hut, having nothing on but a checkered shirt, and a pair of linen drawers, and a pair of pumps on my feet. I got on board the ship as before, and prepared a second raft; and having had experience of the first, I neither made this so unwieldy nor loaded it so hard, but yet I brought away several things very useful to me. At first, in the carpenter's stores, I found two or three bags full of nails and spikes, a great screw-jack, a dozen or two of hatchets, and, above all, that most useful thing called a grindstone. All these I secured together, with several things belonging to the gunner, particularly two or three iron crows, and two barrels of musket bullets, seven muskets, and another fowling-piece, with some small quantity of powder more, a large bag of small shot, and a great roll of sheet lead. But this last was so heavy I could not hoist it up to get it over the ship's side.

Besides these things, I took all the men's clothes that I could find, and a spare fore-topsail, a hammock, and some bedding; and with this I loaded my second raft, and brought them all safe on shore, to my very great comfort.

I was under some apprehensions during my absence from the land that at least my provisions might be devoured on shore; but when I came back I found no sign of any visitor, only there sat a creature like a wild cat upon one of the chests, which, when I came towards it, ran away a little distance, and then stood still. She sat very composed and unconcerned, and looked full in my face, as if she had a mind to be acquainted with me. I presented my gun at her, but as she did not understand it, she was perfectly unconcerned at it, nor did she offer to stir away. Upon which I tossed her a bit of biscuit—though, by the way, I was not very free of it, for my store was not great. However, I spared her a bit, I say, and she went to it, smelled of it, and ate it, and looked, as pleased, for more; but I thanked her, and could spare no more. So she marched off.

Having got my second cargo on shore, though I was fain to open the barrels of powder and bring them by parcels—for they were too heavy, being large casks—I went to work to make me a little tent with the sail and some poles which I cut for that purpose; and into this tent I brought everything that I knew would spoil either with rain or sun, and I piled all the empty chests and casks up in a circle round the tent, to fortify it from any sudden attempt either from man or beast.

When I had done this, I blocked up the door of the tent with some boards within, and an empty chest set up on end without, and spreading one of the beds upon the ground, laying my two pistols just at my head, and my gun at length by me, I went to bed for the first time, and slept very quietly all night, for I was very weary and heavy; for the night before I had slept little, and had laboured very hard all day, as well to fetch all those things from the ship as to get them on shore.

I had the biggest magazine of all kinds now that ever were laid up, I believe, for one man; but I was not satisfied still, for while the ship sat upright in that posture, I thought I ought to get everything out of her that I could; so every day at low water I went on board and brought away some thing or other. But particularly the third time I went I brought away as much of the rigging as I could, as also all the small ropes and rope-twine I could get, with a piece of spare canvas, which was to mend the sails upon occasion, the barrel of wet gunpowder; in a word, I brought away all the sails first and last, only that I was fain to cut them in pieces and bring as much at a time as I could, for they were no more useful to be sails, but as mere canvas only.

But that which confronted me more still was, that at last of all, after I had made five or six voyages as these, and thought I had nothing more to expect from the ship that was worth my meddling with—I say, after all this, I found a great hogshead of bread* and three large runlets of rum or spirits, and a box of sugar, and a barrel of fine flour. This was surprising to me, because I had given over expecting any more provisions, except what was spoiled by the water. I soon emptied the hogshead of that bread, and wrapped it up parcel by parcel in pieces of the sails, which I cut

---

* Biscuits are called ship's "bread".

out; and, in a word, I got all this safe on shore also.

The next day I made another voyage, and now having plundered the ship of what was portable and fit to hand out, I began with the cables; and cutting the great cable into pieces such as I could move, I got two cables and a hawser on shore, with all the ironwork I could get; and having cut down the sprit-sailyard, and the mizzen-yard, and everything I could to make a large raft, I loaded it with all those heavy goods and came away. But my good luck began now to leave me; for this raft was so unwieldy and so overladen, that after I was entered the little cove where I had landed the rest of my goods, not being able to guide it so handily as I did the other, it overset, and threw me and all my cargo into the water. As for myself it was no great harm, for I was near the shore; but as to my cargo, it was great part of it lost, especially the iron, which I expected would have been of great use to me. However, when the tide was out, I got most of the pieces of cable ashore and some of the iron, though with infinite labour: for I was fain to dip for it into the water, a work which fatigued me very much. After this I went every day on board, and brought away what I could get.

I had been now thirteen days on shore, and had been eleven times on board the ship, in which time I had brought away all that one pair of hands could well be supposed capable to bring. But preparing the twelfth time to go on board, I found the wind begin to rise. However, at low water I went on board; and though I thought I had rummaged the cabin so effectually as that nothing more could be found, yet I discovered a locker with drawers in it in one of which I found two or three razors and one pair of large scissors, with some ten or a dozen of good knives and forks; in another I found about thirty-six pounds value in money, some European coin, some Brazil, some pieces of eight, some gold, some silver.

I smiled to myself at the sight of this money. "Oh drug!" said I aloud, "what art thou good for? Thou art not worth to me, no not the taking off of the ground; one of those knives is worth all this heap. I have no manner of use for thee; even remain where thou art, and go to the bottom as a creature whose life is not worth saving." However, upon second thoughts, I took it away, and wrapping all this in a piece of canvas, I began to think of making another raft; but while I was preparing this I found the sky overcast, and the wind began to rise, and in a quarter of an hour it blew a fresh gale from the shore. It presently occurred to me that it was in vain to pretend to make a raft with the wind off shore, and that it was my business to be gone before the tide of flood began, otherwise I might not be able to reach the shore at all. Accordingly I let myself down into the water, and swam across the channel which lay between the ship and the sands and even that with difficulty enough, partly with the weight of the things I had about me, and partly the roughness of the water, for the wind rose very hastily, and before it was quite high water it blew a storm.

But I was gotten home to my little tent, where I lay with all my wealth about me very secure. It blew very hard all that night; and in the morning when I looked out, behold, no more ship was to be seen! I was a little surprised, but recovered myself with this satisfactory reflection, namely, that I had lost no time nor abated any diligence to get everything out of her that could be useful to me, and that indeed there was little left in her that I was able to bring away if I had had more time.

My thoughts were now wholly employed about securing myself against either savages, if any should appear, or wild beasts, if any were in the island; and I had many thoughts of the method how to do this, and what kind of dwelling to make, whether I should make me a cave in the earth or a tent upon the earth.

I consulted several things in my situation which I found would be proper for me. First, health, and fresh water. Secondly, shelter from the heat of the sun. Thirdly, security from ravenous creatures, whether men or beasts. Fourthly, a view to the sea, that if God sent any ship in sight I might not lose any advantage for my deliverance, of which I was not willing to banish all my expectation yet.

In search of a place proper for this, I found a little plain on the side of a rising hill, whose front towards this little plain was steep as a house side, so that nothing could come down upon me from the top. On the side of this rock there was a hollow place worn a little way in like the entrance or door of a cave; but there was not really any cave or way into the rock at all.

On the flat of the green, just before this hollow place, I resolved to pitch my tent. This plain was not above an hundred yards broad, and about twice as long, and lay like a green before my door, and at the end of it descended irregularly every way down into the low grounds by the sea-side. It was on the north-north-west side of the hill, so that I was sheltered from the heat every day till it came to a west and by south sun, or thereabouts, which in those countries is near the setting.

Before I set up my tent I drew a half-circle before the hollow place, which took in about ten yards in its semi-diameter from the rock, and twenty yards in its diameter from its beginning and ending. In this half-circle I pitched two rows of strong stakes driving them into the ground till they stood very firm like piles, the biggest end being out of the ground about five foot and a half, and sharpened on the top. The two rows did not stand above six inches from one another.

Then I took the pieces of cable which I had cut in

the ship, and laid them in rows one upon another within the circle, between these two rows of stakes up to the top, placing other stakes in the inside, leaning against them, about two foot and a half high, like a spur to a post; and this fence was so strong that neither man nor beast could get into it or over it. The entrance into this place I made to be, not by a door, but by a short ladder to go over the top; which ladder, when I was in, I lifted over after me.

Into this fence or fortress, with infinite labour I carried all my riches, all my provisions, ammunition, and stores, of which you have the account above. And I made me a large tent, which, to preserve me from the rains that in one part of the year are very violent there, I made double—namely one smaller tent within, and one larger tent above it, and covered the uppermost with a large tarpaulin which I had saved among the sails. And now I lay no more for a while in the bed which I had brought on shore, but in a hammock. Into this tent I brought all my provisions and everything that would spoil by the wet. When I had done this, I began to work my way into the rock, and bringing all the earth and stones that I dug down out through my tent, I laid them up within my fence in the nature of a terrace, that so it raised the ground within about a foot and a half; and thus I made me a cave just behind my tent, which served me like a cellar to my house.

It cost me much labour and many days before all these things were brought to perfection, and therefore I must go back to some other things which took up some of my thoughts. At the same time it happened after I had laid my scheme for the setting up my tent, and making the cave, that a storm of rain falling from a thick dark cloud, a sudden flash of lightning happened, and after that a great clap of thunder, as is naturally the effect of it. I was not so much surprised with the lightning as I was with a thought which darted into my mind as swift as the lightning itself—O, my powder! My very heart sank within me when I thought that at one blast all my powder might be destroyed, on which not my defence only, but the providing me food, as I thought, entirely depended. I was nothing near so anxious about my own danger, though had the powder taken fire, I had never known who had hurt me.

Such impression did this make upon me, that after the storm was over I laid aside all my works, and applied myself to make bags and boxes to separate the powder and keep it a little and a little in a parcel, in hope that whatever might come it might not all take fire at once, and to keep it so apart that it should not be possible to make one part fire another. I finished this work in about a fortnight; and I think my powder, which in all was about two hundred and forty pounds weight, was divided in not less than a hundred parcels. As to the barrel that had been wet, I did not apprehend any danger from that; so I placed it in my new cave, which in my fancy I called my kitchen.

In the interval of time while this was doing I went out once at least every day with my gun as well to divert myself as to see if I could kill anything fit for food, and as near as I could to acquaint myself with what the island produced. The first time I went out I presently discovered that there were goats in the island—which was a great satisfaction to me; but then it was attended with this misfortune to me, namely, that they were so shy, so subtle, and so swift of foot, that it was the difficultest thing in the world to come at them. But I was not discouraged at this, not doubting but I might now and then shoot one, as it soon happened; for after I had found their haunts a little, I laid wait in this manner for them: I observed if they saw me in the valleys, though they were upon the rocks, they would run away as in a terrible fright; but if they were feeding in the valleys, and I was upon the rocks, they took no notice of me. So afterwards I took this method: I always climbed the rocks first, to get above them, and then had frequently a fair mark. The first shot I made among these creatures I killed a she-goat which had a little kid by her which she gave suck to, which grieved me heartily. But when the old one fell, the kid stood stock-still by her till I came and took her up; and not only so, but when I carried the old one with me upon my shoulders, the kid followed me quite to my enclosure: upon which I laid down the dam and took the kid in my arms, and carried it over my pale, in hopes to have it bred up tame; but it would not eat, so I was forced to kill it and eat it myself. These two supplied me with flesh a great while, for I ate sparingly, and saved my provisions (my bread especially) as much as possibly I could.

And I must not forget, that we had in the ship a dog and two cats of whose eminent history I may have occasion to say something in its place; for I carried both the cats with me; and as for the dog he jumped out of the ship of himself, and swam on shore to me the day after I went on shore with my first cargo, and was a trusty servant to me many years. I wanted nothing that he could fetch me nor any company that he could make up to me; I only wanted to have him talk to me, but that would not do.

And now I began to apply myself to make such necessary things as I found I most wanted, as particularly a chair and a table. I had never handled a tool in my life, and yet in time, by labour, application, and contrivance, I found at last that I wanted nothing but I could have made it, especially if I had had tools. However, I made abundance of things, even without tools, and some with no more tools than an adze and a hatchet, which perhaps were never made that way before, and that with infinite labour. For example, if I wanted a board I had no other way but to cut down a tree, set it on an edge before me, and hew it flat on either side with my axe, till I had brought it to be thin as a plank, and then dubb it smooth with my adze. It is true, by this method I could make but one board out of a whole tree, but this I had no remedy for but patience any more than I had for the prodigious deal of time and labour which it took me up to make a plank or board. But my time or labour was little worth, and so it was as well employed one way as another.

However, I made me a table and a chair, as I observe above, in the first place, and this I did out of the short pieces of boards that I brought on my raft from the ship. But when I had wrought out some boards, as above, I made large shelves of the breadth of a foot and a half, one over another, all along one side of my cave, to lay all my tools, nails, and iron-work, and, in a word, to separate everything at large in their places, that I might come easily at them. I knocked pieces into the wall of the rock to hang my guns and all things that would hang up.

And now it was when I began to keep a journal of every day's employment, until, having no more ink, I was forced to leave it off.

All this time I worked very hard, the rains hindering me many days, nay, sometimes weeks together. When this wall was finished, and the outside double fenced with a turf wall raised up close to it, I persuaded myself that if any people were to come on shore there, they would not perceive anything like a habitation. And it was very well I did so, as may be observed hereafter upon a very remarkable occasion.

During this time I made my rounds in the woods for game every day when the rain admitted me, and made frequent discoveries in these walks of something or other to my advantage. Particularly I found a kind of wild pigeons, who built not as wood-pigeons, in a tree, but rather as house-pigeons, in the holes of the rocks; and taking some young ones, I endeavoured to breed them up tame, and did so; but when they grew older they flew all away, which perhaps was at first for want of feeding them, for I had nothing to give them. However, I frequently found their nests, and got their young ones, which were very good meat.

And now, in the managing my household affairs, I found myself wanting in many things, which I thought at first was impossible for me to make, as indeed as to some of them it was. For instance, I could never make a cask to be hooped. I had a small runlet or two, as I observed before, but I could never arrive to the capacity of making one by them, though I spent many weeks about it. I could neither put in the heads, nor joint the staves so true to one another as to make them hold water. So I gave that also over.

In the next place, I was at a great loss for candle; so that as soon as ever it was dark, which was generally by seven o'clock, I was obliged to go to bed. The only remedy I had was, that when I had killed a goat I saved the tallow; and with a little dish made of clay, which I baked in the sun, to which I added a wick of some oakum, I made me a lamp, and this gave me light, though not a clear, steady light like a candle. In the middle of all my labours it happened that, rummaging my things, I found a little bag, which, as I hinted before, had been filled with corn for the feeding of poultry, not for this voyage, but before, as I suppose, when the ship came from Lisbon. What little remainder of corn had been in the bag was all devoured with the rats, and I saw nothing in the bag but husks and dust; and being willing to have the bag for some other use, I shook the husks of corn out of it on one side of my fortification under the rock. It was a little before the great rains just now mentioned that I threw this stuff away, taking no notice of anything, and not so much as remembering that I had thrown anything there, when, about a month after, or thereabouts, I saw some few stalks of something green shooting out of the ground, which I fancied might be some plant I had not seen;

but I was surprised and perfectly astonished when, after a longer time, I saw about ten or twelve ears come out, which were perfect green barley, of the same kind as our English barley.

This touched my heart a little, and brought tears out of my eyes; and I began to bless myself that such a prodigy of nature should happen upon my account. And this was the more strange to me, because I saw near it still all along by the side of the rock some other straggling stalks, which proved to be stalks of rice, and which I knew because I had seen it grow in Africa when I was ashore there.

I not only thought these the pure productions of Providence for my support, but not doubting but that there was more in the place, I went all over that part of the island where I had been before, peering in every corner and under every rock to see for more of it; but I could not find any. At last it occurred to my thoughts that I had shaken a bag of chickens' meat out in that place, and then the wonder began to cease; and I must confess my religious thankfulness to God's providence began to abate too upon the discovering that all this was nothing but what was common; though I ought to have been as thankful for so strange and unforeseen providence as if it had been miraculous.

I carefully saved the ears of this corn, you may be sure, in their season, which was about the end of June; and laying up every corn, I resolved to sow them all again, hoping in time to have some quantity sufficient to supply me with bread. But it was not till the fourth year that I could allow myself the least grain of this corn to eat, and even then but sparingly. Besides this barley, there was, as above, twenty or thirty stalks of rice, which I preserved with the same care, and whose use was of the same kind or to the same purpose—namely, to make me bread, or rather food, for I found ways to cook it up without baking, though I did that also after some time.

I worked excessively hard these three or four months to get my wall done; and the 14th of April I closed it up, contriving to go into it, not by a door, but over the wall by a ladder, that there might be no sign in the outside of my habitation.

The very next day after this wall was finished I had almost had all my labour overthrown at once, and myself killed. The case was thus: As I was busy in the inside of it, behind my tent, just in the entrance into my cave, I was terribly frightened with a most dreadful surprising thing indeed, for all on a sudden I found the earth come crumbling down from the roof of my cave and from the edge of the hill over my head, and two of the posts I had set up in the cave cracked in a frightful manner. I was heartily scared, but thought nothing of what was really the cause—only thinking that the top of my cave was falling in, as some of it had done before; and for fear

I should be buried in it, I ran forward to my ladder, and not thinking myself safe there neither, I got over my wall for fear of the pieces of the hill which I expected might roll down upon me. I was no sooner stepped down upon the firm ground but I plainly saw it was a terrible earthquake, for the ground I stood on shook three times at about eight minutes' distance with three such shocks as would have overturned the strongest building that could be supposed to have stood on the earth; and a great piece of the top of a rock, which stood about half a mile from me, next the sea, fell down with such a terrible noise as I never heard in all my life. I perceived also the very sea was put into violent motion by it, and I believe the shocks were stronger under the water than on the island.

I was so amazed with the thing itself—having never felt the like or discoursed with anyone that had—that I was like one dead or stupefied; and the motion of the earth made my stomach sick, like one that was tossed at sea. But the noise of the falling of the rock awaked me, as it were, and rousing me from the stupefied condition I was in, filled me with horror, and I thought of nothing then but the hill falling upon my tent and all my household goods, and burying all at once; and this sunk my very soul within me a second time.

After the third shock was over, and I felt no more

for some time, I began to take courage; and yet I had not heart enough to go over my wall again, for fear of being buried alive, but sat still upon the ground, greatly cast down and disconsolate, not knowing what to do.

While I sat thus, I found the air overcast and grow cloudy, as if it would rain. Soon after that the wind rose by little and little, so that in less than half an hour it blew a most dreadful hurricane. The sea was all on a sudden covered over with foam and froth, the shore was covered with the breach of the water, the trees were torn up by the roots, and a terrible. storm it was; and this held about three hours and then began to abate, and in two hours more it was calm and began to rain very hard.

This violent rain forced me to a new work— namely, to cut a hole through my new fortification like a sink to let the water go out, which would else have drowned my cave. After I had been in my cave some time and found still no more shocks of the earthquake follow, I began to be more composed.

It continued raining all that night and great part of the next day, so that I could not stir abroad; but my mind being more composed, I began to think of what I had best do, concluding that if the island was subject to these earthquakes there would be no living for me in a cave, but I must consider of building me some little hut in an open place which I might surround with a wall as I had done here, and so make myself secure from wild beasts or men, but concluded, if I stayed where I was, I should certainly, one time or other, be buried alive.

With these thoughts I resolved to remove my tent from the place where it stood, which was just under the hanging precipice of the hill, and which, if it should be shaken again, would certainly fall upon my tent. And I spent the two next days, being the 19th and 20th of April, in contriving where and how to remove my habitation.

In the meantime it occurred to me that it would require a vast deal of time for me to do this, and that I must be contented to run the venture where I was till I had formed a camp for myself, and had secured it so as to remove to it. This was the 21st.

The next morning I began to consider of means to put this resolve in execution, but I was at a great loss about my tools. I had three large axes and abundance of hatchets (for we carried the hatchets for traffic with the Indians), but with much chopping and cutting knotty hard wood they were all full of notches and dull; and though I had a grindstone, I could not turn it and grind my tools too. This cost me as much thought as a statesman would have bestowed upon a grand point of politics, or a judge upon the life and death of a man.

At length I contrived a wheel with a string to turn it with my foot, that I might have both my hands at liberty.

In the morning, looking towards the sea-side, the tide being low, I saw something lie on the shore bigger than ordinary, and it looked like a cask. When I came to it, I found a small barrel and two or three pieces of the wreck of the ship, which were driven on shore by the late hurricane; and looking towards the wreck itself, I thought it seemed to lie higher out of the water than it used to do.

When I came down to the ship I found it strangely removed. The forecastle, which lay before buried in sand, was heaved up at least six foot; and the stern, which was broken to pieces and parted from the rest by the force of the sea soon after I had left rummaging her, was tossed, as it were, up and cast on one side; and the sand was thrown so high on that side next her stern, that whereas there was a great place of water before, so that I could not come within a quarter of a mile of the wreck without swimming, I could now walk quite up to her when the tide was out.

This wholly diverted my thoughts from the design of removing my habitation; and I busied myself nightly in searching whether I could make any way into the ship; but I found nothing was to be expected of that kind, for that all the inside of the ship was choked up with sand. However, as I had learned not to despair of anything, I resolved to pull everything to pieces that I could of the ship, concluding that everything I could get from her would be of some use or other to me.

May 3.—I began with my saw and cut a piece of a beam through, which I thought held some of the upper part or quarter-deck together; and when I had cut it through I cleared away the sand as well as I could from the side which lay highest; but the tide coming in, I was obliged to give over for that time.

May 4.—I went a-fishing, but caught not one fish that I durst eat of, till I was weary of my sport; when just going to leave off, I caught a young dolphin. I had made me a long line of some rope yarn, but I had no hooks, yet I frequently caught fish enough, as much as I cared to eat; all which I dried in the sun, and ate them dry.

May 5.—Worked on the wreck, cut another beam asunder, and brought three great fir planks off from the decks, which I tied together, and made swim on shore when the tide of flood came on.

May 6.—Worked on the wreck, got several iron bolts out of her, and other pieces of iron-work, worked very hard, and came home very much tired and had thoughts of giving it over.

May 7.—Went to the wreck again, but with an intent not to work; but found the weight of the wreck had broken itself down, the beams being cut that several pieces of the ship seemed to lie loose, and the inside of the hold lay so open that I could see into it, but almost full of water and sand.

I continued this work every day to the 15th of June, except the time necessary to get food, which I always appointed, during this part of my employment, to be when the tide was up, that I might be ready when it was ebbed out; and by this time I had gotten timber and plank and iron-work enough to have built a good boat, if I had known how; and also, I got at several times and in several pieces, near one hundredweight of the sheet lead.

June 16.—Going down to the sea-side I found a large tortoise or turtle.

June 17.—I spent in cooking the turtle. I found in her threescore eggs; and her flesh was to me at that time the most savoury and pleasant that ever I tasted in my life, having had no flesh but of goats and fowls since I landed in this horrid place.

June 18.—Rained all day, and I stayed within. I thought at this time the rain felt cold, and I was something chilly, which I knew was not usual in that latitude.

June 19.—Very ill and shivering, as if the weather had been cold.

June 20.—No rest all night, violent pains in my head, and feverish.

June 21.—Very ill. Frightened almost to death with the apprehensions of my sad condition—to be sick and no help.

June 22.—A little better, but under dreadful apprehensions of sickness.

June 23.—Very bad again, cold and shivering, and then a violent headache.

June 24.—Much better.

June 25.—An ague, very violent. Cold fit and hot with faint sweats after it.

June 26.—Better; and having no victuals to eat, took my gun, but found myself very weak. However, I killed a she-goat, and with much difficulty got it home, and broiled some of it and ate.

June 27.—The ague again, so violent that I lay abed all day, and neither ate nor drank. I was ready to perish for thirst, but so weak I had not strength to stand up or to get myself any water to drink. I suppose I did nothing else for two or three hours, till the fit wearing off I fell asleep, and did not wake till far in the night. When I waked I found myself much refreshed, but weak and exceeding thirsty. However, as I had no water in my whole habitation I was forced to lie till morning, and went to sleep again. In this second sleep I had this terrible dream:

I thought that I was sitting on the ground on the outside of my wall, and that I saw a man descend from a great black cloud, in a bright flame of fire, and light upon the ground. He was all over as bright as a flame so that I could but just bear to look towards him. His countenance was most inexpressibly dreadful, impossible for words to describe When he stepped upon the ground with his feet, I thought the earth trembled, just as it had done before in the earthquake; and all the air looked, to my apprehension, as if it had been filled with flashes of fire. He was no sooner landed upon the earth but he moved forward towards me, with a long spear or weapon in his hand, to kill me. And when he came to a rising ground at some distance, he spoke to me, or I heard a voice so terrible that it is impossible to express the terror of it. All that I can say I understood was this, "Seeing all these things have not brought thee to repentance, now thou shalt die." At which words I thought he lifted up the spear that was in his hand to kill me.

No one that shall ever read this account will expect that I should be able to describe the horrors of my soul at this terrible vision. I mean, that even while it was a dream, I even dreamed of those horrors. Nor is it any more possible to describe the impression that remained upon my mind when I awaked and found it was but a dream.

June 28.—Having been somewhat refreshed with the sleep I had had, and the fit being entirely off, I got up; and though the fright and terror of my dream was very great, yet I considered that the fit of the ague would return again the next day, and now was my time to get something to refresh and support myself when I should be ill. And the first thing I did, I filled a large square case-bottle with water, and set it upon my table in reach of my bed; and to take off the chill or anguish disposition of the water, I put about a quarter of a pint of rum into it and mixed them together. Then I got me a piece of the goat's flesh and broiled it on the coals, but could eat very little. I walked about, but was very weak and withal very sad and heavy-hearted in the sense of my miserable condition, dreading the return of my distemper the next day. At night I made my supper of three of the turtle's eggs, which I roasted in the ashes and ate, as we call it, in the shell: and this was the first bit of meat I had ever asked God's blessing to, even as I could remember, in my whole life.

After I had eaten I tried to walk, but found myself so weak that I could hardly carry the gun, so I went but a little way, and sat down upon the ground, looking out upon the sea, which was just before me, and very calm and smooth.

I drank rum in which I had steeped tobacco, which was so strong and rank of the tobacco that indeed I could scarce get it down. Immediately upon this I went to bed. I found presently it flew up in my head violently, but I fell into a sound sleep, and waked no more till, by the sun, it must necessarily be near three o'clock in the afternoon the next day. Nay, to this hour I am partly of the opinion that I slept all the next day and night, and till almost three that day after; for otherwise I knew not how I should lose a day out of my reckoning in the days of the week, as it appeared some years after I had done. When I awaked I found myself exceedingly refreshed and my spirits lively and cheerful; when I got up I was stronger than I was the day before, and my stomach better, for I was hungry; and, in short, I had no fit the next day, but continued much altered for the better. This was the 29th.

The 30th was my well-day, of course, and I went abroad with my gun, but did not care to travel too far. I killed a sea-fowl or two, something like a brand-goose,* and brought them home, but was not very forward to eat them; so I ate some more of the turtle's eggs, which were very good. This evening I renewed the medicine which I had supposed did me good the day before—namely, the tobacco steeped in rum; only I did not take so much as before, nor did I chew any of the leaf or hold my head over the smoke.

July 3.—I missed the fit for good and all, though I did not recover my full strength for some weeks after.

My condition began now to be, though not less

* Or brent-goose, so called from its burnt or ashen-grey colour.

miserable as to my way of living, yet much easier to my mind; and my thoughts being directed, by a constant reading the Scripture and praying to God, to things of a higher nature, I had a great deal of comfort within, which till now I knew nothing of. Also as my health and strength returned, I bestirred myself to furnish myself with everything that I wanted, and make my way of living as regular as I could.

From the 4th of July to the 14th I was chiefly employed in walking about with my gun in my hand, a little and a little at a time, as a man that was gathering up his strength after a fit of sickness; for it is hardly to be imagined how low I was, and to what weakness I was reduced.

I had been now in this unhappy island above ten months; all possibility of deliverance from this condition seemed to be entirely taken from me, and I firmly believed that no human shape had ever set foot upon that place. Having now secured my habitation, as I thought, fully to my mind, I had a great desire to make a more perfect discovery of the island, and to see what other productions I might find which I yet knew nothing of.

It was the 15th of July that I began to take a more particular survey of the island itself. I went up the creek first, where, as I hinted, I brought my rafts on shore. I found after I came about two miles up that the tide did not flow any higher, and that it was no more than a little brook of running water, and very fresh and good; but this being the dry season there was hardly any water in some parts of it, at least not enough to run in any stream so as it could be perceived. On the bank of this brook I found many pleasant savannahs or meadows, plain, smooth, and covered with grass; and on the rising parts of them, next to the higher grounds where the water, as it might be supposed, never overflowed, I found a great deal of tobacco, green, and growing to a great and very strong stalk. There were divers other plants which I had no notion of or understanding about, and might perhaps have virtues of their own which I could not find out.

I searched for the cassava root, which the Indians in all that climate make their bread of, but I could find none. I saw large plants of aloes, but did not then understand them. I saw several sugar canes, but wild, and for want of cultivation imperfect.

The next day, the 16th, I went up the same way again, and after going something farther than I had gone the day before, I found the brook and the savannahs began to cease, and the country became more woody than before. In this part I found different fruits, and particularly I found melons upon the ground in great abundance, and grapes upon the trees; the vines had spread indeed over the trees, and the clusters of grapes were just now in their prime, very ripe and rich. This was a surprising discovery, and I was exceeding glad of them; but I was warned by my experience to eat sparingly of them, remembering that when I was ashore in Barbary, the eating of grapes killed several of our Englishmen, who were slaves there, by throwing them into fluxes and fevers. But I found an excellent use for these grapes, and that was to cure or dry them in the sun, and keep them as dried grapes or raisins are kept.

I spent all that evening there, and went not back to my habitation, which, by the way, was the first night, as I might say, I had lain from home. In the night I took my first contrivance, and got up into a tree, where I slept well; and the next morning proceeded upon my discovery, travelling near four miles, as I might judge by the length of the valley, keeping still due north, with a ridge of hills on the south and north side of me.

At the end of this march I came to an opening where the country seemed to descend to the west, and a little spring of fresh water, which issued out of the side of the hill by me, ran the other way, that is due east; and the country appeared so fresh, so green, so nourishing, everything being in a constant verdure or flourish of spring, that it looked like a planted garden.

I descended a little on the side of that delicious vale, surveying it with a secret kind of pleasure (though mixed with my other afflicting thoughts)—to think that this was all my own, that I was king and lord of all this country indefeasibly, and had a right of possession; and if I could convey it, I might have it in inheritance as completely as any lord of a manor in England. I saw here abundance of cocoa trees, orange, and lemon, and citron trees, but all wild, and very few bearing any fruit, at least not then. However, the green limes that I gathered were not only pleasant to eat, but very wholesome; and I mixed their juice afterwards with water, which made it very wholesome, and very cool, and refreshing.

I found now I had business enough to gather and carry home, and I resolved to lay up a store, as well of grapes as limes and lemons, to furnish myself for the wet season, which I knew was approaching.

In order to this, I gathered a great heap of grapes in one place and a lesser heap in another place, and a great parcel of limes and lemons in another place; and, taking a few of each with me, I travelled homeward, and resolved to come again and bring a bag or sack, or what I could make to carry the rest home.

Accordingly, having spent three days in this journey, I came home;—so I must now call my tent and my cave. But before I got thither the grapes were spoiled—the richness of the fruits and the weight of the juice having broken them and bruised them, they were good for little or nothing; as to the limes, they were good, but I could bring but a few.

The next day, being the 19th, I went back, having made me two small bags to bring home my harvest. But I was surprised when, coming to my heap of grapes, which were so rich and fine when I gathered them I found them all spread about, trod to pieces and dragged about, some here, some there, and abundance eaten and devoured. By this I concluded there were some wild creatures thereabouts which had done this, but what they were I knew not.

However, as I found that there was no laying them up on heaps, and no carrying them away in a sack, but that one way they would be destroyed, and the other way they would be crushed with their own weight, I took another course; for I gathered a large quantity of the grapes and hung them up upon the out branches of the trees, that they night cure and dry in the sun; and as for the limes and lemons, I carried as many back as I could well stand under.

When I came home from this journey I contemplated with great pleasure the fruitfulness of that valley and the pleasantness of the situation, the security from storms on that side of the water, and the wood, and concluded that I had pitched upon a place to fix my abode which was by far the worst part of the country. Upon the whole I began to consider of removing my habitation and to look out for a place equally safe as where I now was situate, if possible, in that pleasant, fruitful part of the island.

This thought ran long in my head, and I was exceeding fond of it for some time, the pleasantness of the place tempting me; but when I came to a nearer view of it, and to consider that I was now by the seaside, where it was at least possible that something might happen to my advantage, and by the same ill fate that brought me hither might bring some other unhappy wretches to the same place; and though it was scarce probable that any such thing should ever happen, yet to enclose myself among the hills and woods in the centre of the island was to anticipate my bondage, and to render such an affair not only improbable but impossible; and that, therefore, I ought not by any means to remove.

However, I was so enamoured of this place that I spent much of my time there for the whole remaining part of the month of July; and though, upon second thoughts, I resolved as above not to remove, yet I built me a little kind of a bower and surrounded it at a distance with a strong fence, being a double hedge, as high as I could reach, well staked and filled between with brushwood; and here I lay very secure, sometimes two or three nights together, always going over it with a ladder as before; so that I fancied now I had my country house and my sea-coast house. And this work took me up to the beginning of August.

I had but newly finished my fence and begun to enjoy my labour, but the rains came on, and made me stick close to my first habitation. For though I had made me a tent like the other, with a piece of a sail, and spread it very well, yet I had not the shelter of a hill to keep me from storms, nor a cave behind me to retreat into when the rains were extraordinary.

About the beginning of August, as I said, I had finished my bower and began to enjoy myself. The 3rd of August I found the grapes I had hung up were perfectly dried, and indeed were excellent good raisins of the sun; so I began to take them down from the trees, and it was very happy that I did so, for the rains which followed would have spoiled them, and I had lost the best part of my winter food, for I had above two hundred large bunches of them. No sooner had I taken them all down, and carried most of them home to my cave, but it began to rain, and from hence, which was the 14th of August, it rained more or less every day till the middle of October.

In this season I was much surprised with the increase of my family. I had been concerned for the loss of one of my cats, who ran away from me, or as I thought had been dead, and I heard no more tale or tidings of her till, to my astonishment, she came home about the end of August with three kittens! But from these three cats I afterwards came to be so pestered with cats that I was forced to kill them like vermin or wild beasts, and to drive them from my house as much as possible.

From the 14th of August to the 26th incessant rain, so that I could not stir, and was now very careful not to be much wet. In this confinement I began to be straitened for food, but venturing out twice I one day killed a goat, and the last day, which was the 26th, found a very large tortoise, which was a treat to me; and my food was regulated thus:—I eat a bunch of raisins for my breakfast, a piece of the goat's flesh or of the turtle for my dinner broiled— for to my great misfortune I had no vessel to boil or stew anything—and two or three of the turtle's eggs for my supper.

During this confinement in my cover by the rain I worked daily two or three hours at enlarging my cave and by degrees worked it on towards one side till I came to the outside of the hill, and made a door or way out, which came beyond my fence or wall, and so I came in and out this way. But I was not perfectly easy at lying so open; for as I had managed myself before, I was in a perfect enclosure, whereas now I thought I lay exposed and open for anything to come in upon me. And yet I could not perceive that there was any living thing to fear, the biggest creature that I had yet seen upon the island being a goat.

September the 30th.—I was now come to the unhappy anniversary of my landing. I cast up the notches on my post, and found I had been on shore 365 days. I kept this day as a solemn fast, setting it apart to religious exercise.

A little after this my ink began to fail me, and so I contented myself to use it more sparingly, and to write down only the most remarkable events of my life, without continuing a daily memorandum of other things.

The rainy season and the dry season began now to appear regular to me; and I learned to divide them, so as to provide for them accordingly. But I bought all my experience before I had it; and this I am going to relate was one of the most discouraging experiments that I made at all. I have mentioned that I had saved the few ears of barley and rice which I had so surprisingly found springing up, as I thought of themselves, and believe there were about thirty stalks of rice, and about twenty of barley. And now I thought it a proper time to sow it after the rains, the sun being in its southern position going from me.

Accordingly I dug up a piece of ground as well as I could with my wooden spade, and dividing it into two parts, I sowed my grain; but as I was sowing it casually occurred to my thoughts that I would not sow it all at first, because I did not know when was the proper time for it, so I sowed about two-thirds of the seed, leaving about a handful of each.

It was a great comfort to me afterwards that I did so, for not one grain of that I sowed this time came to anything; for the dry months following, the earth having had no rain after the seed was sown, it had no moisture to assist its growth, and never came up at all till the wet season had come again, and then it grew as if it had been but newly sown.

Finding my first seed did not grow, which I easily imagined was by the drought, I sought for a more moist piece of ground to make another trial in; and I dug up a piece of ground near my new bower, and sowed the rest of my seed in February, a little before the vernal equinox, and this having the rainy months of March and April to water it, sprung up very pleasantly and yielded a very good crop. But having part of the seed left only, and not daring to sow all that I had, I had but a small quantity at last, my whole crop not amounting to above half a peck of each kind.

But by this experiment I was made master of my business, and knew exactly when the proper season was to sow; and that I might expect two seed-times and two harvests every year.

While this corn was growing I made a little discovery, which was of use to me afterwards. As soon as the rains were over and the weather began to settle, which was about the month of November, I made a visit up the country to my bower, where, though I had not been some months, yet I found all things just as I left them. The circle, or double hedge, that I had made was not only firm and entire, but the stakes, which I had cut out of some trees that grew thereabouts, were all shot out and grown with long branches, as much as a willow-tree usually shoots the first year after lopping its head. I could not tell what tree to call it that these stakes were cut from. I was surprised and yet very well pleased to see the young trees grow; and I pruned them, and led them up to grow as much alike as I could; and it is scarce credible how beautiful a figure they grew into in three years. So that, though the hedge made a circle of about twenty-five yards in diameter, yet the trees (for such I might now call them) soon covered it; and it was a complete shade, sufficient to lodge under all the dry season.

This made me resolve to cut some more stakes, and make me a hedge like this in a semicircle round my wall—I mean that of my first dwelling—which I did; and placing the trees or stakes in a double row, at about eight yards' distance from my first fence, they grew presently, and were at first a fine cover to my habitation, and afterwards served for a defence also, as I shall observe in its order.

I found now that the seasons of the year might generally be divided, not into summer and winter, as in Europe, but into the rainy seasons and the dry seasons. The rainy season sometimes held longer or shorter, as the winds happened to blow, but this was the general observation I made. After I had found by experience, the ill consequence of being abroad in the rain, I took care to furnish myself with provisions beforehand that I might not be obliged to go out, and I sat within doors as much as possible during the wet months.

In this time I found much employment (and very suitable also to the time), for I found great occasion of many things which I had no way to furnish myself with but by hard labour and constant application; particularly I tried many ways to make myself a basket, but all the twigs I could get for the purpose proved so brittle that they would do nothing. It proved of excellent advantage to me now, that when I was a boy I used to take great delight in standing at a basketmaker's in the town where my father lived, to see them make their wicker-ware; and being, as boys usually are, very officious to help, and a great observer of the manner how they worked those things, and sometimes lending a hand, I had by this means full knowledge of the methods of it, that I wanted nothing but the materials, when it came into my mind that the twigs of that tree from whence I cut my stakes that grew might possibly be as tough as the sallows, and willows, and osiers in England, and I resolved to try.

Accordingly the next day I went to my country-house, as I called it, and cutting some of the smaller twigs, I found them to my purpose as much as I could desire; whereupon I came the next time prepared with a hatchet to cut down a quantity, which I soon found, for there was great plenty of them. These I set up to dry within my circle or hedge, and when they were fit for use I carried them to my cave, and here during the next season I employed myself in making, as well as I could, a great many baskets, both to carry earth, or to carry or lay up anything as I had occasion; and though I did not finish them very handsomely, yet I made them sufficiently serviceable for my purpose.

Having mastered this difficulty, and employed a world of time about it, I bestirred myself to see if possible how to supply two wants. I had no vessels to hold anything that was liquid except two runlets, which were almost full of rum, and some glass bottles, some of the common size, and others which were case-bottles square, for the holding of water, spirits, &c. I had not so much as a pot to boil anything, except a great kettle, which I saved out of the ship, and which was too big for such use as I designed—namely, to make broth, and stew a bit of meat by itself. The second thing I would fain have had was a tobacco-pipe, but it was impossible to me to make one; however I found a contrivance for that too at last.

I employed myself in planting my second row of stakes or piles and in this wicker-working all the summer or dry season, when another business took me up more time than it could be imagined I could spare.

I mentioned before that I had a great mind to see the whole island, and that I had travelled up the brook. I now resolved to travel quite across to the sea-shore on that side; so taking my gun, a hatchet, and my dog, and a larger quantity of powder and shot than usual, with two biscuit-cakes and a great bunch of raisins in my pouch for my store, I began my journey. When I had passed the vale where my bower stood as above, I came within view of the sea to the west, and it being a very clear day I fairly descried land, whether an island or a continent I could not tell; but it lay very high. By my guess it could not be less than fifteen or twenty leagues off. I could not tell what part of the world this might be, otherwise than that I knew it must be part of America, and, as I concluded by all my observations, must be near the Spanish dominions; and perhaps was all inhabited by savages, where, if I should have landed, I had been in a worse condition than I was now.

Besides, after some pause upon this affair, I considered that if this land was the Spanish coast, I should certainly, one time or other, see some vessel pass or repass one way or other; but if not, then it was the savage coast between the Spanish country and Brazil, which are indeed the worst of savages, for they are cannibals, or men-eaters.

With these considerations I walked very leisurely forward. I found that side of the island where I now was much pleasanter than mine; the open or savanna fields sweet, adorned with flowers and grass, and full of very fine woods. I saw abundance of parrots, and fain I would have caught one, if possible, to have kept it to be tame, and taught it to speak to me. I did, after some painstaking, catch a young parrot, for I knocked it down with a stick, and having recovered it I brought it home; but it was some years before I could make him speak. However, at last I taught him to call me by my name very familiarly. But the accident that followed, though it be a trifle, will be very diverting in its place.

I was exceedingly diverted with this journey. I found in the low grounds hares, as I thought them to be, and foxes; but they differed greatly from all the other kinds I had met with, nor could I satisfy myself to eat them, though I killed several. But I had no need to be venturous, for I had no want of food, and of that which was very good too; especially these three sorts—namely, goats, pigeons, and turtle or tortoise, which, added to my grapes, Leadenhall Market could not have furnished a table better than I in proportion to the company.

As soon as I came to the sea-shore I was surprised to see that I had taken up my lot on the worst side of the island; for here, indeed, the shore was covered with innumerable turtles, whereas on the other side I had found but three in a year and a half. Here was also an infinite number of fowls of many kinds; some which I had seen, and some which I had not seen of before—and many of them very good meat—but such as I knew not the names of, except those called penguins. I could have shot as many as I pleased, but was very sparing of my powder and shot.

I confess this side of the country was much pleasanter than mine; but yet I had not the least inclination to remove, for as I was fixed in my habitation, it became natural to me, and I seemed all the while I was here to be as it were upon a journey, and from home. However, I travelled along the shore of the sea towards the east, I suppose about twelve miles; and then, setting up a great pole upon the shore for a mark, I concluded I would go home again, and that the next journey I took should be on the other side of the island east from my dwelling, and so round till I came to my post again: of which in its place.

I took another way to come back than that I went, thinking I could easily keep all the island so much in my view that I could not miss finding my first dwelling by viewing the country. But I found myself mistaken; for being come about two or three miles I found myself descended into a very large valley, but so surrounded with hills, and those hills covered with wood, that I could not see which was my way by any direction but that of the sun, nor even then, unless I knew very well the position of the sun at that time of the day.

It happened, to my farther misfortune, that the weather proved hazy for three or four days while I was in this valley; and not being able to see the sun I wandered about very uncomfortably, and at last was obliged to find out the sea-side, look for my post, and come back the same way I went. And then by easy journeys I turned homeward, the weather being exceedingly hot, and my gun, ammunition, hatchet, and other things very heavy.

In this journey my dog surprised a young kid, and seized upon it, and I running in to take hold of it, caught it, and saved it alive from the dog. I had a great mind to bring it home if I could; for I had often been musing whether it might not be possible to get a kid or two, and so raise a breed of tame goats, which might supply me when my powder and shot should be all spent.

I made a collar to this little creature, and with a string which I made of some rope yarn, which I always carried about me, I led him along, though with some difficulty, till I came to my bower; and there I enclosed him and left him, for I was very impatient to be at home, from whence I had been absent above a month. I cannot express what a satisfaction it was to me to come into my old hutch and lie down in my hammock-bed.

I reposed myself here a week, to rest and regale myself after my long journey; during which most of the time was taken up in the weighty affair of making a cage for my poll, who began now to be a mere domestic, and to be mighty well acquainted with me. Then I began to think of the poor kid which I had penned in within my little circle, and resolved to go and fetch it home or give it some food. Accordingly I went, and found it where I left it; for, indeed, it could not get out, but almost starved for want of food. I went and cut boughs of trees and branches of such shrubs as I could find, and threw it over; and having fed it, I tied it as I did before, to lead it away. But it was so tame with being hungry that I had no need to have tied it, for it followed me like a dog; and as I continually fed it, the creature became so loving, so gentle, and so fond that it became from that time one of my domestics also, and would never leave me afterwards.

The rainy season of the autumnal equinox was now come, and I kept the 30th of September in the same solemn manner as before, being the anniversary of my landing on the island, having now been there two years, and no more prospect of being delivered than the first day I came there.

I cannot say that after this, for five years, any extraordinary thing happened to me, but I lived on in the same course, in the same posture and place, just as before. The chief things I was employed in besides my yearly labour of planting my barley and rice and curing my raisins, of both which I always kept up just enough to have sufficient stock of one year's provisions beforehand; I say, besides this yearly labour and my daily labour of going out with my gun, I had one labour to make me a canoe, which at last I finished; so that, by digging a canal to it of six feet wide and four feet deep, I brought it into the creek almost half a mile. As for the first, which was so vastly big, as I made it without considering beforehand, as I ought to do, how I should be able to launch it, so never being able to bring it to the water, or bring the water to it, I was obliged to let it lie where it was, as a memorandum to teach me to be wiser next time. Indeed, the next time, though I could not get a tree proper for it, and in a place where I could not get the water to it at any less distance than as I have said, near half a mile; yet, as I saw it was practicable at last, I never gave it over; and though I was near two years about it, yet I never grudged my labour, in hopes of having a boat to go off to sea at last.

However, though my little periagua was finished, yet the size of it was not at all answerable to the design which I had in view when I made the first—I mean, of venturing over to the *terra firma*, where it was above forty miles broad. Accordingly, the smallness of my boat assisted to put an end to that design; and now I thought no more of it. But as I had a boat, my next design was to make a tour round the island.

For this purpose, that I might do everything with discretion and consideration, I fitted up a little mast to my boat, and made a sail to it out of some of the pieces of the ship's sail.

Having fitted my mast and sail, and tried the boat, I found she would sail very well. Then I made little lockers, or boxes, at either end of my boat, to put provisions, necessaries, and ammunition, &c., into, to be kept dry either from rain or the spray of the sea; and a little long hollow place I cut in the inside of the boat, where I could lay my gun, making a flap to hang down over it to keep it dry.

I fixed my umbrella also in a step at the stern, like a mast, to stand over my head, and keep the heat of the sun off me like an awning; and thus I every now and then took a little voyage upon the sea, but never went far out, not far from the little creek. But at last, being eager to view the circumference of my little kingdom, I resolved upon my tour, and accordingly I victualled my ship for the voyage, putting in two dozen of my loaves of barley bread, an earthen pot full of parched rice, a little bottle of rum, half a goat, and powder and shot for killing more, and two large watch-coats of those which I had saved out of the seamen's chests: these I took, one to lie upon, and the other to cover me in the night.

It was the 6th of November, in the sixth year of my reign, or my captivity, which you please, that I set out on this voyage, and I found it much longer than I expected. For though the island itself was not very large, yet, when I came to the east side of it, I found a great ledge of rocks lie out above two leagues into the sea, some above water, some under it; and beyond that a shoal of sand, lying dry half a league more. So that I was obliged to go a great way out to sea to double the point.

When first I discovered them I was going to give over my enterprise and come back again, not knowing how far it might oblige me to go out to sea and above all, doubting how I should get back again; so I came to an anchor—for I had made me a kind of an anchor with a piece of a broken grapling, which I got out of the ship.

Having secured my boat, I took my gun and went on shore, climbing up upon a hill which seemed to overlook that point, where I saw the full extent of it and resolved to venture.

In my viewing the sea from that hill where I stood I perceived a strong, and indeed a most furious current, which ran to the east, and even came close to the point. And I took the more notice of it, because I saw there might be some danger that when I came into it I might be carried out to sea by the strength of it, and not be able to make the island again. And indeed, had I not gotten first up upon this hill, I believe it would have been so; for there was the same current on the other side the island, only that it set off at a farther distance. And I saw there was a strong eddy under the shore; so I had nothing to do but to get in out of the first current, and I should presently be in an eddy.

The third day, in the morning, the wind having abated overnight, the sea was calm, and I ventured. But I am a warning piece again to all rash and ignorant pilots; for no sooner was I come to the point, when even I was not my boat's length from the shore, but I found myself in a great depth of water and a current like the sluice of a mill. It carried my boat along with it with such violence that all I could do could not keep her so much as on the edge of it; but I found it hurried me farther and farther out from the eddy, which was on my left hand. There was no wind stirring to help me; and all I could do with my paddlers signified nothing. And now I began to give myself over for lost; for as the current was on both sides the island, I knew in a few leagues' distance they must join again, and then I was irrecoverably gone. Nor did I see any possibility of avoiding it; so that I had no prospect before me but of perishing—

not by the sea, for that was calm enough, but of starving for hunger. I had, indeed, found a tortoise on the shore as big almost as I could lift, and had tossed it into the boat; and I had a great jar of fresh water—that is to say, one of my earthen pots; but what was all this to being driven into the vast ocean, where, to be sure, there was no shore, no mainland or island for a thousand leagues at least!

It is scarce possible to imagine the consternation I was now in, being driven from my beloved island (for so it appeared to me now to be) into the wide ocean, almost two leagues, and in the utmost despair of ever recovering it again. However, I worked hard, till indeed my strength was almost exhausted, and kept my boat as much to the northward—that is, towards the side of the current which the eddy lay on—as possibly I could; when about noon, as the sun passed the meridian, I thought I felt a little breeze of wind in my face, springing up from the south-south-east. This cheered my heart a little, and especially when in about half an hour more it blew a pretty small gentle gale. By this time I was gotten at a frightful distance from the island, and had the least cloud or hazy weather intervened, I had been undone another way too; for I had no compass on board, and should never have known how to have steered towards the island if I had but once lost sight of it. But the weather continuing clear, I applied myself to get up my mast again, and spread my sail, standing away to the north as much as possible to get out of the current.

Just as I had set my mast and sail, and the boat began to stretch away, I saw even by the clearness of the water some alteration of the current was near; for where the current was so strong the water was foul; but perceiving the water clear, I found the current abate, and presently I found to the east, at about half a mile, a breach of the sea upon some rocks. These rocks, I found, caused the current to part again.

They who know what it is to have a reprieve brought to them upon the ladder, or to be rescued from thieves just going to murder them, or who have been in such like extremities, may guess what my present surprise of joy was, and how gladly I put my boat into the stream of this eddy, and, the wind also freshening, how gladly I spread my sail to it, running cheerfully before the wind, and with a strong tide or eddy under foot.

This eddy carried me about a league in my way back again directly towards the island, but about two leagues more to the northward than the current which carried me away at first; so that when I came near the island I found myself open to the northern shore of it—that is to say, the other end of the island opposite to that which I went out from.

When I had made something more than a league of way by the help of this current or eddy, I found it was spent, and served me no farther. However, I found that being between the two great currents, namely, that on the south side, which had hurried me away, and that on the north, which lay about a league on the other side: I say, between these two, in the wake of the island, I found the water at least still and running no way; and having still a breeze of wind fair for me, I kept on steering directly for the island, though not making such fresh way as I did before.

About four o'clock in the evening, being then within about a league of the island, I found the point of the rocks which occasioned this disaster stretching out, as is described before, to the southward, and casting off the current more southwardly had of course made another eddy to the north, and this I found very strong, but not directly setting the way my course lay, which was due west, but almost full north. However, having a fresh gale, I stretched across this eddy slanting north-west, and in about an hour came within about a mile of the shore, where, it being smooth water, I soon got to land.

I was now at a great loss which way to get home with my boat. I had run so much hazard, and knew too much the case to think of attempting it by the way I went out; and what might be at the other side

(I mean the west side) I knew not, nor had I any mind to run any more ventures; so I only resolved in the morning to make my way westward along the shore, and to see if there was no creek where I might lay up my frigate in safety, so as to have her again if I wanted her. In about three mile or thereabout, coasting the shore, I came to a very good inlet or bay about a mile over, which narrowed till it came to a very little rivulet or brook, where I found a very convenient harbour for my boat, and where she lay as if she had been in a little dock made on purpose for her. Here I put in, and having stowed my boat very safe, I went on shore to look about me and see where I was.

I soon found I had but a little passed by the place where I had been before, when I travelled on foot to that shore; so taking nothing out of my boat but my gun and my umbrella, for it was exceeding hot, I began my march. The way was comfortable enough after such a voyage as I had been upon, and I reached my old bower in the evening, where I found everything standing as I left it; for I always kept it in good order, being, as I said before, my country house.

I got over the fence and laid me down in the shade to rest my limbs, for I was very weary, and fell asleep. But judge you, if you can, that read my story, what a surprise I must be in when I was waked out of my sleep by a voice calling me by my name several times: "Robin, Robin, Robin Crusoe; poor Robin Crusoe! Where are you, Robin Crusoe? Where are you? Where have you been?"

I was so dead asleep at first, being fatigued with rowing, or paddling, as it is called, the first part of the day, and with walking the latter part, that I did not wake thoroughly; but dozing between sleeping and waking, thought I dreamed that somebody spoke to me. But as the voice continued to repeat, "Robin Crusoe, Robin Crusoe", at last I began to wake more perfectly, and was at first dreadfully frightened, and started up in the utmost consternation. But no sooner were my eyes open but I saw my Poll sitting on the top of the hedge, and immediately knew that it was he that spoke to me; for just in such bemoaning language I had used to talk to him, and teach him; and he had learned it so perfectly that he would sit upon my finger and lay his bill close to my face, and cry, "Poor Robin Crusoe, where are you? Where have you been? How come you here?" and such things as I had taught him.

However, even though I knew it was the parrot, and that indeed it could be nobody else, it was a good while before I could compose myself: first, I was amazed how the creature got thither, and then how he should just keep about the place and no-where else. But as I was well satisfied it could be nobody but honest Poll, I got it over; and holding out my hand, and calling him by his name Poll, the sociable creature came to me, and sat upon my thumb, as he used to do, and continued talking to me, "Poor Robin Crusoe," and "How did I come here?" and "Where had I been?" just as if he had been over-joyed to see me again; and so I carried him home along with me.

I had now had enough of rambling to sea for some time, and had enough to do for many days to sit still and reflect upon the danger I had been in. I would have been very glad to have had my boat again on my side of the island; but I knew not how it was practicable to get it about; so I contented myself to be without any boat, though it had been the product of so many months' labour to make it; and of so many more to get it unto the sea. In this government of my temper I remained near a year—lived a very sedate, retired life, as you may well suppose.

I improved myself in this time in all the mechanic exercises which my necessities put me upon apply-ing myself to, and I believe could, upon occasion, make a very good carpenter, especially considering how few tools I had. Besides this, I arrived at an unexpected perfection in my earthenware, and con-trived well enough to make them with a wheel, which I found infinitely easier and better; because I made things round and shapeable, which before were filthy things indeed to look on. But I think I was never more vain of my own performance, or more joyful for anything I found out, than for my being able to make a tobacco-pipe. And though it was a very ugly clumsy thing when it was done, and only burned red like other earthenware, yet, as it was hard and firm and would draw the smoke, I was exceedingly comforted with it

In my wicker-ware, also, I improved much, and made abundance of necessary baskets, as well as my invention showed me. Though not very handsome, yet they were such as were very handy and convenient for my laying things up in, or fetching things home in.

I began now to perceive my powder abated considerably, and this was a want which it was impossible for me to supply, and I began seriously to consider what I must do when I should have no more powder; that is to say, how I should do to kill any goat.

But being now in the eleventh year of my residence, and, as I have said, my ammunition growing low, I set myself to study some art to trap and snare the goats, to see whether I could not catch some of them alive, and particularly I wanted a she-goat.

To this purpose I made snares to hamper them; and I believe they were more than once taken in them; but my tackle was not good, for I had no wire, and I always found them broken, and my bait devoured. At length I resolved to try a pit-fall. So I dug several large pits in the earth, in places where I had observed the goats used to feed; and over these pits I placed hurdles of my own making too, with a great weight upon them. And several times I put ears of barley and dry rice, without setting the trap; and I could easily perceive that the goats had gone in and eaten up the corn, for I could see the mark of their feet. At length I set three traps in one night; and going the next morning, I found them all standing, and yet the bait eaten and gone. This was very discouraging. However, I altered my trap; and, not to trouble you with particulars, going one morning to see my trap, I found in one of them a large old he-goat; and in one of the other, three kids—a male and two females.

As to the old one, I knew not what to do with him; he was so fierce I durst not go into the pit to him—that is to say, to go about to bring him away alive, which was what I wanted. I could have killed him; but that was not my business, nor would it answer my end. So I even let him out, and he ran away as if he had been frighted out of his wits. But I had forgot then what I learned afterwards—that hunger will tame a lion. If I had let him stay there three or four days without food, and then have carried him some water to drink, and then a little corn, he would have been as tame as one of the kids—for they are mighty sagacious, tractable creatures where they are well used.

However, for the present I let him go, knowing no better at that time. Then I went to the three kids; and taking them one by one, I tied them with strings together, and with some difficulty brought them all home.

But then it presently occurred to me that I must keep the tame from the wild, or else they would always run wild when they grew up. And the only way for this was to have some enclosed piece of ground, well fenced either with hedge or pale, to keep them in so effectually, that those within might not break out, or those without break in. This was a great undertaking for one pair of hands. Yet, as I saw there was an absolute necessity for doing it, my first piece of work was to find out a proper piece of ground—namely, where there was likely to be herbage for them to eat, water for them to drink, and cover to keep them from the sun.

I pitched upon a place very proper for all these, being a plain open piece of meadow-land or savanna (as our people call it in the western colonies), which had two or three little rills of fresh water in it, and at one end was very woody. For the first beginning I resolved to enclose a piece of about one hundred and fifty yards in length and one hundred yards in breadth; which, as it would maintain as many as I should have in any reasonable time, so, as my flock increased, I could add more ground to my enclosure.

I was about three months hedging in the first piece; and till I had done it I tethered the three kids in the best part of it, and used them to feed as near me as possible, to make them familiar; and very often I would go and carry them some ears of barley or a handful of rice, and feed them out of my hand; so that after my enclosure was finished, and I let them loose, they would follow me up and down, bleating after me for a handful of corn. This answered my end. And in about a year and a half I had a flock of about twelve goats—kids and all; and in two years more I had three-and-forty—besides several that I took and killed for my food. And after that I enclosed five several pieces of ground to feed them in, with little pens to drive them into, to take them as I wanted, and gates out of one piece of ground into another. But this is not all; for now I not only had goat's flesh to feed on when I pleased, but milk too—a thing which, indeed, in my beginning I did not so much as think of, and which, when it came into my thoughts, was really an agreeable surprise. For now I set up my dairy, and had sometimes a gallon or two of milk in a day. And as Nature, who gives supplies of food to every creature, dictates even naturally how to make use of it; so I that had never milked a cow, much less a goat, or seen butter or cheese made, very readily and handily, though after a great many essays and miscarriages, made me both butter and cheese at last, and never wanted for it afterwards.

It would have made a Stoic smile to have seen me and my little family sit down to dinner. There was my Majesty, the prince and lord of the whole island. I had the lives of all my subjects at my absolute command—I could hang, draw, give liberty, and take it away; and no rebels among all my subjects.

Then to see how like a king I dined, too, all alone attended by my servants. Poll, as if he had been my favourite, was the only person permitted to talk to me. My dog, who was now grown very old and crazy, sat always at my right hand; and two cats, one on one side the table and one on the other expecting now and then a bit from my hand as a mark of special favour.

I was something impatient, as I have observed, to have the use of my boat—though very loath to run any more hazards; and therefore sometimes I sat contriving ways to get her about the island, and at other times I sat myself down contented enough without her. But I had a strange uneasiness in my mind to go down to the point of the island where, as I have said, in my last ramble I went up the hill to see how the shore lay and how the current set, that I might see what I had to do. This inclination increased upon me every day, and at length I resolved to travel thither by land, following the edge of the shore. I did so.

But had anyone in England been to meet such a man as I was, it must either have frighted them or raised a great deal of laughter. And as I frequently stood still to look at myself, I could not but smile at the notion of my travelling through Yorkshire with such an equipage and in such a dress. Be pleased to take a sketch of my figure as follows.

I had a great high shapeless cap made of a goat's skin, with a flap hanging down behind, as well to keep the sun from me as to shoot the rain off from running into my neck, nothing being so hurtful in these climates as the rain upon the flesh under the clothes.

I had a short jacket of goat-skin, the skirts coming down to about the middle of my thighs; and a pair of open-kneed breeches of the same—the breeches were made of the skin of an old he-goat, whose hair hung down such a length on either side, that like pantaloons it reached to the middle of my legs; stockings and shoes I had none, but had made me a pair of somethings, I scarce know what to call them, like buskins, to flap over my legs and lace on either side like spatterdashes, but of a most barbarous shape—as indeed were all the rest of my clothes.

I had on a broad belt of goat-skin dried, which I

---

* *Frog*, a tassel or small bobbin of silk, cloth, or braid used instead of a button by passing over it a loop which is sewn to the other side of the coat. The word is derived from the Portuguese *froco*, a tuft or flock of wool or silk.

drew together with two thongs of the same, instead of buckles, and in a kind of a frog* on either side of this. Instead of a sword and a dagger hung a little saw and hatchet, one on one side, one on the other. I had another belt not so broad, and fastened in the same manner, which hung over my shoulder; and at the end of it, under my left arm, hung two pouches, both made of goat's skin too—in one of which hung my powder, in the other my shot. At my back I carried my basket, on my shoulder my gun, and over my head a great clumsy, ugly goat-skin umbrella— but which, after all, was the most necessary thing I had about me, next to my gun. As for my face, the colour of it was really not so Mulatto-like as one might expect from a man not at all careful of it, and living within nineteen degrees of the equinox. My beard I had once suffered to grow till it was about a quarter of a yard long; but as I had both scissors and razors sufficient I had cut it pretty short, except what grew on my upper lip, which I had trimmed into a large pair of Mohammedan whiskers, such as I had seen worn by some Turks whom I saw at Salee; for the Moors did not wear such, though the Turks did. Of these moustaches or whiskers I will not say they were long enough to hang my hat upon them, but they were of a length and shape monstrous enough, and such as in England would have passed for frightful.

But all this is by-the-by. For as to my figure, I had

so few to observe me that it was of no manner of consequence, so I say no more to that part. In this kind of figure I went my new journey, and was out five or six days. I travelled first along the seashore, directly to the place where I first brought my boat to an anchor to get up upon the rocks; when looking forward to the point of the rocks which lay out, I was surprised to see the sea all smooth and quiet—no rippling, no motion, no current any more there than in other places. I was at a strange loss to understand this, and resolved to spend some time in the observing it, to see if nothing from the sets of the tide had occasioned it; but I was presently convinced how it was—namely, that the tide of ebb setting from the west, and joining with the current of waters from some great river on the shore, must be the occasion of this current, and that according as the wind blew more forcibly from the west or from the north, this current came near or went farther from the shore. For waiting thereabouts till evening, I went up to the rock again; and then the tide of ebb being made, I plainly saw the current again as before, only that it ran farther off.

This observation convinced me that I had nothing to do but to observe the ebbing and the flowing of the tide, and I might very easily bring my boat about the island again.

But now I come to a new scene of my life. It

happened one day about noon, going towards my boat, I was exceedingly surprised with the print of a man's naked foot on the shore, which was very plain to be seen in the sand. I stood like one thunder-struck, or as if I had seen an apparition. I listened, I looked round me; I could hear nothing, nor see any-thing. I went up to a rising ground to look farther. I went up the shore and down the shore; but it was all one, I could see no other impression but that one. I went to it again to see if there were any more, and to observe if it might not be my fancy; but there was no room for that, for there was exactly the very print of a foot, toes, heel, and every part of a foot;—how it came thither I knew not, nor could in the least imagine. But after innumerable fluttering thoughts, like a man perfectly confused and out of myself, I came home to my fortification, not feeling, as we say, the ground I went on, but terrified to the last degree, looking behind me at every two or three steps, mistaking every bush and tree, and fancying every stump at a distance to be a man. Nor is it possible to describe how many various shapes affrighted imagination represented things to me in; how many wild ideas were found every moment in my fancy, and what strange unaccountable whimsies came into my thoughts by the way.

When I came to my castle, for so I think I called it ever after this, I fled into it like one pursued. Whether

I went over by the ladder as first contrived, or went in at the hole in the rock which I called a door, I cannot remember; no, nor could I remember the next morning; for never had frightened hare fled to cover or fox to earth with more terror of mind than I to this retreat.

I slept none that night. The farther I was from the occasion of my fright the greater my apprehensions were, which is something contrary to the nature of such things, and especially to the usual practice of all creatures in fear. But I was so embarrassed with my own frightful ideas of the thing, that I formed nothing but dismal imaginations to myself, even though I was now a great way off it. Sometimes I fanced it must be the devil, and reason joined in with me upon this supposition. For how should any other thing in human shape come into the place? Where was the vessel that brought them? What marks were there of any other footsteps? And how was it possible a man should come there? But, then, to think that Satan should take human shape upon him in such a place, where there could be no manner of occasion for it but to leave the print of his foot behind him, and that even for no purpose, too, for he could not be sure I should see it; this was an amusement the other way. I considered that the devil might have found out abundance of other ways to have terrified me than this of the single print of a foot;—

that, as I lived quite on the other side of the island, he would never have been so simple to leave a mark in a place where it was ten thousand to one whether I should ever see it or not; and in the sand, too, which the first surge of the sea upon a high wind would have defaced entirely. All this seemed inconsistent with the thing itself, and with all the notions we usually entertain of the subtlety of the devil.

I presently concluded, then, that it must be some more dangerous creature—namely, that it must be some of the savages of the mainland over against me, who had wandered out to sea in their canoes, and, either driven by the currents or by contrary winds, had made the island.

In the middle of these cogitations, apprehensions, and reflections, it came into my thought one day that all this might be a mere chimera of my own, and that this foot might be the print of my own foot when I came on shore from my boat. This cheered me up a little too, and I began to persuade myself it was all a delusion, that it was nothing else but my own foot; and why might not I come that way from the boat as well as I was going that way to the boat?

Now I began to take courage and to peep abroad again, for I had not stirred out of my castle for three days and nights, so that I began to starve for provision, for I had little or nothing within doors but some barley-cakes and water. Then I knew that my goats wanted to be milked, too, which usually was my evening diversion.

Heartening myself, therefore, with the belief that this was nothing but the print of one of my own feet and so I might be truly said to start at my own shadow, I began to go abroad again, and went to my country house to milk my flock; but to see with what fear I went forward, how often I looked behind me, how I was ready every now and then to lay down my basket and run for my life, it would have made anyone have thought I was haunted with an evil conscience, or that I had been lately most terribly frighted, and so indeed I had.

However, as I went down thus two or three days, and having seen nothing, I began to be a little bolder, and to think there was really nothing in it but my own imagination. But I could not persuade myself fully of this till I should go down to the shore again and see this print of a foot and measure it by my own, and see if there was any similitude or fitness that I might be assured it was my own foot. But when I came to the place, *first*, it appeared evidently to me that when I laid up my boat I could not possibly be on shore anywhere hereabout; *secondly*, when I came to measure the mark with my own foot, I found my foot not so large by a great deal. Both these things filled my head with new imaginations, and gave me the vapours again to the highest degree, so that I shook with cold like one in an ague. And I went home again, filled with the belief that some man or men had been on shore there; or, in short, that the island was inhabited, and I might be surprised before I was aware—and what course to take for my security I knew not.

I took all the measures human prudence could suggest for my own preservation, and it will be seen at length that they were not altogether without just reason, though I foresaw nothing at that time more than my mere fear suggested to me.

After I had secured one part of my little living stock, I went about the whole island searching for another private place to make such another deposit, when, wandering more to the west point of the island than I had ever done yet, and looking out to sea, I thought I saw a boat upon the sea at a great distance. I had found a prospective-glass or two in one of the seamen's chests which I saved out of our ship; but I had it not about me, and this was so remote that I could not tell what to make of it, though I looked at it till my eyes were not able to hold to look any longer. Whether it was a boat or not I do not know; but as I descended from the hill I could see no more of it, so I gave it over—only I resolved to go no more out without a prospective-glass in my pocket.

When I was come down the hill to the shore, being the south-west point of the island, I was perfectly confounded and amazed—nor is it possible for me to express the horror of my mind—at seeing the shore spread with skulls, hands, feet, and other bones of human bodies; and particularly I observed a place where there had been a fire made, and a circle dug in the earth like a cock-pit, where it is supposed the savage wretches had sat down to their inhuman feastings upon the bodies of their fellow-creatures.

I was so astonished with the sight of these things that I entertained no notions of any danger to myself from it for a long while. All my apprehensions were buried in the thoughts of such a pitch of inhuman brutality, and the horror of the degeneracy of human nature, which, though I had heard of often, yet I never had so near a view of before. In short, I turned away my face from the horrid spectacle: my stomach grew sick, and I was just at the point of fainting. So I gat me up the hill again with all the speed I could, and walked on towards my habitation.

I entertained such an abhorrence of the savage wretches that I have been speaking of, and of the wretched inhuman custom of their devouring and eating one another up, that I continued pensive and sad, and kept close within my own circle for almost two years after this.

Time, however, and the satisfaction I had that I was in no danger of being discovered by these people, began to wear off my uneasiness about them, and I began to live just in the same composed manner as before—only with this difference, that I used more caution and kept my eyes more about me than I did before, lest I should happen to be seen by any of them; and, particularly, I was more cautious of firing my gun, lest any of them being on the island should happen to hear of it. And it was therefore a very good providence to me that I had furnished myself with a tame breed of goats, that I needed not hunt any more about the woods or shoot at them; and if I did catch any of them after this; it was by traps and snares, as I had done before: so that for two years after this I believe I never fired my gun once off, though I never went out without it. And, which was more, as I had saved three pistols out of the ship, I always carried them out with me—or at least two of them—sticking them in my goat-skin belt; also I furbished up one of the great cutlasses that I had out of the ship, and made me a belt to put on also, so that I was now a most formidable fellow to look at when I went abroad, if you add to the former description of myself the particular of two pistols, and a great broadsword hanging at my side in a belt, but without a scabbard.

Things going on thus, as I have said, for some time, I seemed, excepting these cautions, to be reduced to my former calm, sedate way of living. All these things tended to showing me more and more how far my condition was from being miserable, compared to some others; nay, to many other particulars of life which it might have pleased God to have made my lot.

However, at last, after many secret disputes with myself, and after great perplexities about it, the eager, prevailing desire of deliverance at length mastered all the rest, and I resolved, if possible, to get one of those savages into my hands, cost what it would.

About a year and half after I had entertained these notions, and by long musing had, as it were, resolved them all into nothing for want of an occasion to put them in execution, I was surprised one morning early with seeing no less than five canoes all on shore together on my side the island, and the people who belonged to them all landed and out of my sight! Having waited a good while, listening to hear if they made any noise, at length, being very impatient, I set my guns at the foot of my ladder, and clambered up to the top of the hill by my two stages, as usual; standing so, however, that my head did not appear above the hill, so that they could not perceive me by any means. Here I observed, by the help of my perspective-glass, that they were no less than thirty in number, that they had a fire kindled, that they had had meat dressed. How they had cooked it, that I knew not, or what it was; but they were all dancing, in I know not how many barbarous gestures and figures, their own way round the fire.

While I was thus looking on them I perceived by my perspective two miserable wretches dragged from the boats, where it seems they were laid by, and were now brought out for the slaughter. I perceived one of them immediately fell, being knocked down, I suppose, with a club or wooden sword—for that was their way—and two or three others were at work immediately cutting him open for their cookery, while the other victim was left standing by himself till they should be ready for him. In that very moment this poor wretch, seeing himself a little at liberty, nature inspired him with hopes of life, and he started away from them, and ran with incredible swiftness along the sands directly towards me; I mean towards that part of the coast where my habitation was.

It came now very warmly upon my thoughts, and indeed irresistibly, that now was my time to get me a servant, and perhaps a companion or assistant; and that I was called plainly by Providence to save this poor creature's life. I immediately run down the ladders with all possible expedition, fetches my two guns, for they were both but at the foot of the ladders, as I observed above, and, getting up again with the same haste to the top of the hill, I crossed towards the sea; and having a very short cut and all down-hill, clapped myself in the way between the pursuers and the pursued, hallooing aloud to him that fled, who, looking back, was at first perhaps as much frighted at me as at them; but I beckoned with my hand to him to come back, and in the meantime I slowly advanced towards the two that followed; then rushing at once upon the foremost, I knocked him down with the stock of my piece. I was loath to fire, because I would not have the rest hear, though at that distance it would not have been easily heard, and being out of sight of the smoke too, they would not have easily known what to make of it. Having knocked this fellow down, the other who pursued with him stopped as if he had been frighted, and I advanced apace towards him; but as I came nearer I perceived presently he had a bow and arrow, and was fitting it to shoot at me; so I was then necessitated to shoot at him first, which I did, and killed him at the first shoot. The poor savage who fled, but had stopped, though he saw both his enemies fallen and killed, as he thought, yet was so frighted with the fire and noise of my piece that he stood stockstill, and neither came forward nor went backward, though he seemed rather inclined to fly still than to come on. I hallooed again to him, and made signs to come forward, which he easily understood, and came a little way, then stopped again, and then a little farther, and stopped again, and I could then perceive that he stood trembling, as if he had been taken pris-

oner and had just been to be killed as his two enemies were. I beckoned him again to come to me,
and gave him all the signs of encouragement that I
could think of, and he came nearer and nearer, kneel-
ing down every ten or twelve steps in token of ac-
knowledgment for my saving his life. I smiled at
him, and looked pleasantly, and beckoned to him to
come still nearer. At length he came close to me,
and then he kneeled down again, kissed the ground,
and laid his head upon the ground, and taking me by
the foot, set my foot upon his head: this, it seems,
was in token of swearing to be my slave for ever. I
took him up and made much of him, and encouraged
him all I could. But there was more work to do yet;
for I perceived the savage whom I knocked down
was not killed, but stunned, with the blow, and began to come to himself; so I pointed to him, and
showing him the savage, that he was not dead. Upon
this he spoke some words to me, and though I could
not understand them, yet I thought they were pleasant to hear, for they were the first sound of a man's
voice that I had heard, my own excepted, for above
twenty-five years. But there was no time for such
reflections now. The savage who was knocked down
recovered himself so far as to sit up upon the ground,
and I perceived that my savage began to be afraid;
but when I saw that, I presented my other piece at
the man, as if I would shoot him. Upon this my

savage, for so I called him now, made a motion to me to lend him my sword, which hung naked in a belt by my side; so I did. He no sooner had it but he runs to his enemy, and at one blow cut off his head as cleverly, no executioner in Germany could have done it sooner or better; which I thought very strange for one who I had reason to believe never saw a sword in his life before, except their own wooden swords. However, it seems, as I learned afterwards, they made their wooden swords so sharp, so heavy, and the wood is so hard, that they will cut off heads even with them, ay, and arms, and that at one blow too. When he had done this, he comes laughing to me in sign of triumph, and brought me the sword again, and with abundance of gestures, which I did not understand, laid it down with the head of the savage that he had killed just before me.

But that which astonished him most, was to know how I had killed the other Indian so far off. So pointing to him, he made signs to me to let him go to him; so I bade him go as well as I could. When he came to him he stood like one amazed, looking at him, turned him first on one side, then on the other, looked at the wound the bullet had made. He took up his bow and arrows and came back, so I turned to go away, and beckoned to him to follow me, making signs to him that more might come after them. Then I carried him, not to my castle, but quite away to my cave, on the farther part of the island.

He was a comely, handsome fellow, perfectly well made, with straight strong limbs, not too large, tall and well shaped, and as I reckon, about twenty-six years of age. He had a very good countenance, not a fierce and surly aspect; but seemed to have something very manly in his face; and yet he had all the sweetness and softness of a European in his countenance too, especially when he smiled. His hair was long and black, not curled like wool; his forehead very high and large, and a great vivacity and sparkling sharpness in his eyes. The colour of his skin was not quite black, but very tawny; and yet not of an ugly yellow nauseous tawny, as the Brazilians and Virginians and other natives of America are; but of a bright kind of a dun olive colour, that had in it something very agreeable, though not very easy to describe. His face was round and plump; his nose small, not flat like the negroes; a very good mouth, thin lips, and his fine teeth well set, and white as ivory. After he had slumbered, rather than slept about half an hour, he waked again, and comes out of the cave to me, for I had been milking my goats, which I had in the enclosure just by. When he espied me he came running to me, laying himself down again upon the ground, with all the possible signs of a humble thankful disposition, making many antic gestures to show it. In a little time I began to speak to him, and teach him to speak to me. And first, I made him know his name should be Friday, which was the day I saved his life. I likewise taught him to say Master, and then let him know that was to be my name. I likewise taught him to say Yes and No, and to know the meaning of them. I gave him some milk in an earthen pot, and let him see me drink it before him, and sop my bread in it. And I gave him a cake of bread to do the like, which he quickly complied with, and made signs that it was very good for him.

I kept there with him all that night, but as soon as it was day I beckoned to him to come with me, and let him know I would give him some clothes, at which he seemed very glad, for he was stark naked. I then led him up to the top of the hill, to see if his enemies were gone; and, pulling out my glass, I looked and saw plainly the place where they had been, but no appearance of them or of their canoes; so that it was plain that they were gone, and had left their two comrades behind them without any search after them.

But I was not content with this discovery; but having now more courage, and consequently more curiosity, I takes my man Friday with me, giving him the sword in his hand with the bow and arrows at his back, which I found he could use very dexterously, making him carry one gun for me, and I two for myself; and away we marched to the place where these creatures had been, for I had a mind now to get some fuller intelligence of them. When I came to the place, my very blood ran chill in my veins, and my heart sunk within me at the horror of the spectacle. Indeed it was a dreadful sight—at least it was so to me, though Friday made nothing of it. The place was covered with human bones, the ground dyed with their blood, great pieces of flesh left here and there, half-eaten, mangled and scorched; and, in short, all the tokens of the triumphant feast they had been making there after a victory over their enemies. I caused Friday to gather all the skulls, bones, flesh, and whatever remained, and lay them together on a heap, and make a great fire upon it, and burn them all to ashes.

When we had done this, we came back to our castle, and there I fell to work for my man Friday; and first of all I gave him a pair of linen drawers, which I had out of the poor gunner's chest I mentioned, and which I found in the wreck, and which with a little alteration fitted him very well. Then I made him a jerkin of goat-skin as well as my skill would allow, and I was now grown a tolerable good tailor; and I gave him a cap which I had made of a hare-skin, very convenient and fashionable enough; and thus he was clothed for the present tolerably well, and was mighty well pleased to see himself almost as well clothed as his master. It is true, he went awkwardly in these things at first: wearing the drawers was very awkward to him, and the sleeves of the waistcoat galled his shoulders and the inside of his arms; but a little easing them where he complained they hurt him, and using himself to them, at length he took to them very well.

The next day after I came home to my hutch with him, I began to consider where I should lodge him; and that I might do well for him, and yet be perfectly easy myself, I made a little tent for him in the vacant place between my two fortifications, in the inside of the last, and in the outside of the first. And as there was a door or entrance there into my cave, I made a formal framed doorcase, and a door to it of boards, and set it up in the passage, a little within the entrance; and causing the door to open on the inside, I barred it up in the night, taking in my ladders too; so that Friday could no way come at me in the inside of my innermost wall without making so much noise in getting over, that it must needs waken me. For my first wall had now a complete roof over it of long poles covering all my tent and leaning up to the side of the hill, which was again laid cross with smaller sticks instead of laths, and then thatched over a great thickness with the rice straw, which was strong like reeds; and at the hole or place which was left to go in or out by the ladder, I had placed a kind of trap-door, which, if it had been attempted on the outside, would not have opened at all, but would have fallen down and made a great noise; and as to weapons, I took them all in to my side every night.

But I needed none of all this precaution; for never man had a more faithful, loving, sincere servant than Friday was to me, without passions, sullenness, or designs, perfectly obliged and engaged; his very affections were tied to me, like those of a child to a father, and I daresay he would have sacrificed his life for the saving mine upon any occasion whatsoever. The many testimonies he gave me of this put it out of doubt, and soon convinced me that I needed to use no precautions as to my safety on his account.

I began now to consider that, having two mouths to feed instead of one, I must provide more ground for my harvest, and plant a larger quantity of corn than I used to do; so I marked out a larger piece of land, and began the fence in the same manner as before, in which Friday not only worked very willingly and very hard, but did it very cheerfully. And I told him what it was for; that it was for corn to make more bread, because he was now with me, and that I might have enough for him and myself too. He appeared very sensible of that part, and let me know that he thought I had much more labour upon me on his account than I had for myself; and that he would work the harder for me if I would tell him what to do.

This was the pleasantest year of all the life I led in this place. Friday began to talk pretty well, and understand the names of almost everything I had occasion to call for, and of every place I had to send him to, and talk a great deal to me; so that, in short, I began now to have some use for my tongue again, which indeed I had very little occasion for before— that is to say, about speech. Besides the pleasure of talking to him, I had a singular satisfaction in the fellow himself. His simple unfeigned honesty appeared to me more and more every day, and I began really to love the creature; and, on his side, I believe he loved me more than it was possible for him ever to love anything before.

After Friday and I became more intimately acquainted, and that he could understand almost all I said to him, and speak fluently, though in broken English, to me, I acquainted him with my own story, or at least so much of it as related to my coming into the place, how I had lived there, and how long. I let him into the mystery, for such it was to him, of gunpowder and bullet, and taught him how to shoot. I gave him a knife, which he was wonderfully delighted with; and I made him a belt, with a frog hanging to it, such as in England we wear hangers in; and in the frog, instead of a hanger, I gave him a hatchet, which was not only as good a weapon in some cases, but much more useful upon other occasions.

I showed him the ruins of our boat which we lost

when we escaped, and which I could not stir with my whole strength then, but was now fallen almost all to pieces. Upon seeing this boat Friday stood musing a great while, and said nothing. I asked him what it was he studied upon. At last says he, "Me see such boat like come to place at my nation."

I did not understand him a good while; but at last, when I had examined farther into it, I understood by him that a boat, such as that had been, came on shore upon the country where he lived; that is, as he explained it, was driven thither by stress of weather. I presently imagined that some European ship must have been cast away upon their coast, and the boat might get loose and drive ashore; but was so dull that I never once thought of men making escape from a wreck thither, much less whence they might come; so I only inquired after a description of the boat.

Friday described the boat to me well enough; but brought me better to understand him when he added, with some warmth, "We save the white mans from drown." Then I presently asked him if there were any white mans, as he called them, in the boat. "Yes," he said; "the boat full of white mans." I asked him how many. He told upon his fingers seventeen. I asked him then what became of them. He told me, "They live, they dwell at my nation."

Upon this I inquired of him more critically what

was become of them. He assured me they lived still there; that they had been there about four years that the savages let them alone, and gave them victuals to live. I asked him how it came to pass they did not kill them and eat them. He said, "No, they make brother with them;" that is, as I understood him, a truce. And then he added, "They no eat mans but when make the war fight."

It was after this some considerable time that, being on the top of the hill, at the east side of the island, from whence, as I have said, I had in a clear day discovered the main, or continent of America, Friday, the weather being very serene, looks very earnestly towards the mainland, and in a kind of surprise falls a jumping and dancing, and calls out to me, for I was at some distance from him. I asked him what was the matter. "Oh, joy!" says he, "oh, glad! There see my country, there my nation!"

From this time, I confess, I had a mind to venture over, and see if I could possibly join with these men, who, I made no doubt, were Spaniards or Portuguese; not doubting but, if I could, we might find some method to escape from thence, being upon the continent, and a good company together, better than I could from an island forty miles off the shore and alone without help. So after some days I took Friday to work again, by way of discourse, and told him I would give him a boat to go back to his own nation; and accordingly I carried him to my frigate, which lay on the other side of the island, and having cleared it of water, for I always kept it sunk in the water, I brought it out, showed it him, and we both went into it.

I found he was a most dexterous fellow at managing it, would make it go almost as swift and fast again as I could. So when he was in I said to him, "Well now, Friday, shall we go to your nation?" He looked very dull at my saying so; which it seems was because he thought the boat too small to go so far. I told him then I had a bigger. So the next day I went to the place where the first boat lay which I had made, but which I could not get into water. He said that was big enough. But then, as I had taken no care of it, and it had lain two or three and twenty years there, the sun had split and dried it, that it was in a manner rotten. Friday told me such a boat would do very well, and would carry "much enough vittle, drink, bread;" that was his way of talking.

At last Friday pitched upon a tree, for I found he knew much better than I what kind of wood was fittest for it; nor can I tell, to this day, what wood to call the tree we cut down, except that it was very like the tree we call fustic, or between that and the Nicaragua wood, for it was much of the same colour and smell. Friday was for burning the hollow or cavity of this tree out to make it for a boat; but I showed him how rather to cut it out with tools; which, after I had showed him how to use, he did very handily; and in about a month's hard labour we finished it, and made it very handsome, especially when with our axes, which I showed him how to handle, we cut and hewed the outside into the true shape of a boat. After this, however, it cost us near a fortnight's time to get her along, as it were, inch by inch upon great rollers into the water. But when she was in, she would have carried twenty men with great ease.

When she was in the water, and though she was so big, it amazed me to see with what dexterity and how swift my man Friday would manage her, turn her, and paddle her along; so I asked him if he would, and if we might venture over in her. "Yes," he said; "we venture over in her very well, though great blow wind." However, I had a farther design that he knew nothing of; and that was, to make a mast and sail, and to fit her with an anchor and cable. As to a mast, that was easy enough to get, so I pitched upon a straight young cedar-tree, which I found near the place; and I set Friday to work to cut it down, and gave him directions how to shape and order it. But as to the sail, that was my particular care. I knew I had old sails, or rather pieces of old sails enough; but as I had had them now twenty-six years by me, and had not been very careful to preserve them, not imagin- ing that I should ever have this kind of use for them,

I did not doubt but they were all rotten; and, indeed, most of them were so. However, I found two pieces which appeared pretty good, and with these I went to work, and with a great deal of pains and awkward tedious stitching (you may be sure) for want of needles, I at length made a three-cornered ugly thing, like what we call in England a shoulder-of-mutton sail, to go with a boom at bottom and a little short sprit at the top, such as usually our ships' longboats sail with, and such as I best knew how to manage.

I was near two months performing this last work—namely, rigging and fitting my mast and sails; for I finished them very complete, making a small stay and a sail or fore-sail to it, to assist if we should turn to windward. And, which was more than all, I fixed a rudder to the stern of her to steer with.

After all this was done, too, I had my man Friday to teach as to what belonged to the navigation of my boat; for though he knew very well how to paddle a canoe, he knew nothing what belonged to a sail and a rudder, and was the most amazed when he saw me work the boat to and again in the sea by the rudder; and how the sail jibed, and filled this way or that way, as the course we sailed changed—I say, when he saw this he stood like one astonished and amazed. However, with a little use I made all these things familiar to him; and he became an expert sailor.

I was now entered on the seven-and-twentieth year

of my captivity in this place. The rainy season was in the meantime upon me, when I kept more within doors than at other times. So I had stowed our new vessel as secure as we could, bringing her up into the creek where, as I said, in the beginning I landed my rafts from the ship; and hauling her up to the shore at high-water mark, I made my man Friday dig a little dock, just big enough to hold her, and just deep enough to give her water enough to float in: and then, when the tide was out, we made a strong dam across the end of it to keep the water out; and so she lay dry as to the tide from the sea; and to keep the rain off we laid a great many boughs of trees so thick that she was as well thatched as a house; and thus we waited for the months of November and December, in which I designed to make my adventure.

When the settled season began to come in, as the thought of my design returned with the fair weather, I was preparing daily for the voyage. And the first thing I did was to lay by a certain quantity of provisions, being the stores for our voyage; and intended, in a week or a fortnight's time to open the dock and launch out our boat. I was busy one morning upon something of this kind, when I called to Friday, and bid him go to the seashore and see if he could find a turtle or tortoise—a thing which we generally got once a week for the sake of the eggs as well as the flesh. Friday had not been long gone when he came running back, and flew over my outer wall or fence like one that felt not the ground or the steps he set his feet on; and before I had time to speak to him he cries out to me: "O master! O master!—O sorrow!—O bad!" "What's the matter Friday?" says I. "O—yonder—there," says he, "one, two, three canoe!—one, two, three!" "Well, Friday," says I, "do not be frightened." So I heartened him up as well as I could. However, I saw the poor fellow was most terribly scared; for nothing ran in his head but that they were come to look for him, and would cut him in pieces and eat him; and the poor fellow trembled so that I scarce knew what to do with him. I comforted him as well as I could, and told him I was in as much danger as he, and that they would eat me as well as him: "But," says I, "Friday, we must resolve to fight them. Can you fight, Friday?" "Me shoot," says he; "but there come many great number." "No matter for that," said I again; "our guns will fright them that we do not kill;" so I asked him, "Whether, if I resolved to defend him, he would defend me, and stand by me, and do just as I bid him?" He said, "Me die when you bid die, master." So I went and fetched a good dram of rum and gave him; for I had been so good a husband of my rum that I had a great deal left. When he had drank it, I made him take the two fowling-pieces which we always carried, and load them with large swan-shot, as big as small pistol bullets; then I took four muskets, and loaded them with two slugs and five small bullets each; and my two pistols I loaded with a brace of bullets each; hung my great sword as usual naked by my side, and gave Friday his hatchet.

When I had thus prepared myself I took my perspective-glass and went up to the side of the hill to see what I could discover. And I found quickly, by my glass, that there were one-and-twenty savages, three prisoners, and three canoes; and that their whole business seemed to be the triumphal banquet upon these three human bodies (a barbarous feast indeed), but nothing more than as I had observed was usual with them.

I observed, also, that they were landed, not where they had done when Friday made his escape, but nearer to my creek, where the shore was low, and where a thick wood came close almost down to the sea. This, with the abhorrence of the inhuman errand these wretches came about, filled me with such indignation, that I came down again to Friday and told him I was resolved to go down to them and kill them all; and asked him if he would stand by me? He was now gotten over his fright, and his spirits being a little raised with the dram I had given him, he was very cheerful.

In this fit of fury I took first and divided the arms

which I had charged, as before, between us. I gave Friday one pistol to stick in his girdle, and three guns upon his shoulder; and I took one pistol and the other three myself; and in this posture we marched out. I took a small bottle of rum in my pocket, and gave Friday a large bag with more powder and bullet. And as to orders, I charged him to keep close behind me, and not to stir, or shoot, or do anything till I bid him; and in the meantime not to speak a word. In this posture I fetched a compass to my right hand of near a mile, as well to get over the creek as to get into the wood; so that I might come within shot of them before I should be discovered, which I had seen by my glass it was easy to do.

With this resolution I entered the wood, and with all possible wariness and silence, Friday following close at my heels, I marched till I came to the skirt of the wood, on the side which was next to them; only that one corner of the wood lay between me and them. Here I called softly to Friday, and showing him a great tree, which was just at the corner of the wood, I bade him go to the tree and bring me word if he could see there plainly what they were doing. He did so, and came immediately back to me and told me they might be plainly viewed there; that they were all about their fire eating the flesh of one of their prisoners; and that another lay bound upon the sand, a little from them, which he said they would

kill next, and which fired all the very soul within
me. He told me it was not one of their nation, but
one of the men who he had told me of, white and
bearded, that came to their country in the boat. I was
filled with horror at the very naming the white,
bearded man, and going to the tree I saw plainly by
my glass a white man who lay upon the beach of the
sea, with his hands and his feet tied with flags, or
things like rushes; and that he was a European, and
had clothes on.

I had now not a moment to lose; for nineteen of
the dreadful wretches sat upon the ground, all close
huddled together, and had just sent the other two to
butcher the poor Christian and bring him perhaps
limb by limb to their fire, and they were stooped
down to untie the bands at his feet. I turned to Friday. "Now, Friday," said I, "do as I bid thee." Friday said he would. "Then, Friday," says I, "do exactly as you see me do—fail in nothing." So I set
down one of the muskets and the fowling-piece upon
the ground, and Friday did the like by his; and with
the other musket I took my aim at the savages, bidding him do the like. Then asking him if he was
ready, he said: "Yes." "Then fire at them," said I;
and the same moment I fired also.

Friday took his aim so much better than I, that on
the side that he shot he killed two of them and
wounded three more, and on my side I killed one

and wounded two. They were, you may be sure, in a dreadful consternation; and all of them who were not hurt jumped up upon their feet, but did not immediately know which way to run or which way to look, for they knew not from whence their destruction came. Friday kept his eyes close upon me, that, as I had bid him, he might observe what I did. So as soon as the first shot was made, I threw down the piece and took up the fowling-piece, and Friday did the like; he sees me cock and present; he did the same again. "Are you ready, Friday?" said I. "Yes," says he. "Let fly, then," says I, "in the name of God!" and with that I fired again among the amazed wretches, and so did Friday. And as our pieces were now loaded with what I called swan-shot, or small pistol bullets, we found only two drop; but so many were wounded, that they ran about yelling and screaming like mad creatures, all bloody and miserably wounded, most of them, whereof three more fell quickly after, though not quite dead.

"Now, Friday," says I, laying down the discharged pieces and taking up the musket which was yet loaded, "follow me," says I; which he did with a great deal of courage. Upon which I rushed out of the wood and showed myself, and Friday close at my foot. As soon as I perceived they saw me I shouted as loud as I could, and bade Friday do so too; and running as fast as I could—which, by the way, was not very fast, being laden with arms as I was—I made directly towards the poor victim, who was, as I said, lying upon the beach or shore between the place where they sat and the sea. The two butchers, who were just going to work with him, had left him at the surprise of our first fire, and fled in a terrible fright to the sea-side and had jumped into a canoe, and three more of the rest made the same way. I turned to Friday, and bid him step forward and fire at them. He understood me immediately, and running about forty yards to be near them, he shot at them, and I thought he had killed them all; for I saw them all fall of a heap into the boat, though I saw two of them up again quickly. However, he killed two of them, and wounded the third; so that he lay down in the bottom of the boat as if he had been dead.

While my man Friday fired at them, I pulled out my knife and cut the flags that bound the poor victim, and loosing his hands and feet, I lifted him up, and asked him in the Portuguese tongue, "What he was?" He answered in Latin, "Christianus;" but was so weak and faint that he could scarce stand or speak. I took my bottle out of my pocket and gave it him, making signs that he should drink, which he did; and I gave him a piece of bread, which he eat. Then I asked him, "What countryman he was?" And he said, "Espagniole;" and being a little recovered, let me know, by all the signs he could possibly make, how much he was in my debt for his deliverance. "Seignior," said I, with as much Spanish as I could make up, "we will talk afterwards, but we must fight now. If you have any strength left, take this pistol and sword and lay about you." He took them very thankfully; and no sooner had he the arms in his hands, but, as if they had put new vigour into him, he flew upon his murderers like a fury, and had cut two of them in pieces in an instant. For the truth is, as the whole was a surprise to them, so the poor creatures were so much frighted with the noise of our pieces, that they fell down for mere amazement and fear, and had no more power to attempt their own escape than their flesh had to resist our shot. And that was the case of those five that Friday shot at in the boat, for as three of them fell with the hurt they received, so the other two fell with the fright.

I kept my piece in my hand still, without firing, being willing to keep my charge ready, because I had given the Spaniard my pistol and sword. So I called to Friday, and bade him run up to the tree from whence we first fired, and fetch the arms which lay there that had been discharged—which he did with great swiftness; and then giving him my musket, I sat down myself to load all the rest again, and bade them come to me when they wanted. While I was loading these pieces there happened a fierce engagement between the Spaniard and one of the savages, who made at him with one of their great wooden swords, the same weapon that was to have killed him before if I had not prevented it. The Spaniard, who was as bold and as brave as could be imagined, though weak, had fought this Indian a good while, and had cut him two great wounds on his head; but the savage, being a stout lusty fellow, closing in with him, had thrown him down (being faint), and was wringing my sword out of his hand, when the Spaniard, though undermost, wisely quitting the sword, drew the pistol from his girdle, shot the savage through the body and killed him upon the spot, before I, who was running to help him, could come near him.

Friday, being now left to his liberty, pursued the flying wretches with no weapon in his hand but his hatchet; and with that he despatched those three who, as I said before, were wounded at first and fallen, and all the rest he could come up with. And the Spaniard coming to me for a gun, I gave him one of the fowling-pieces, with which he pursued two of the savages and wounded them both: but as he was not able to run, they both got from him into the wood, where Friday pursued them and killed one of them; but the other was too nimble for him, and though he was wounded, yet had plunged himself into the sea, and swam with all his might off to

those two who were left in the canoe; which three in
the canoe, with one wounded, who we know not
whether he died or no, were all that escaped our
hands of one-and-twenty. Running to one of their canoes, I jumped in and bade Friday follow me; but when
I was in the canoe I was surprised to find another poor
creature lie there alive, bound hand and foot.

I immediately cut the twisted flags, or rushes, which
they had bound him with, and would have helped
him up; but he could not stand or speak, but groaned
most piteously, believing, it seems still, that he was
only unbound in order to be killed.

When Friday came to him, I bade him speak to
him and tell him of his deliverance, and, pulling out
my bottle, made him give the poor wretch a dram,
which, with the news of his being delivered, revived
him, and he sat up in the boat. But when Friday
came to hear him speak, and look in his face, it
would have moved anyone to tears to have seen how
Friday kissed him, embraced him, hugged him, cried,
laughed, hallooed, jumped about, danced, sung, then
cried again, wrung his hands, beat his own face and
head, and then sung and jumped about again like a
distracted creature. It was a good while before I could
make him speak to me, or tell me what was the
matter; but when he came a little to himself he told
me that it was his father!

I observed the poor affectionate creature every two

minutes, or perhaps less, all the while he was here, turned his head about, to see if his father was in the same place and posture as he left him sitting; and at last he found he was not to be seen; at which he started up, and without speaking a word, flew with that swiftness to him, that one could scarce perceive his feet to touch the ground as he went. But when he came, he only found he had laid himself down to ease his limbs; so Friday came back to me presently, and I then spoke to the Spaniard to let Friday help him up if he could, and lead him to the boat, and then he should carry him to our dwelling, where I would take care of him. But Friday, a lusty strong fellow, took the Spaniard quite up upon his back, and carried him away to the boat, and set him down softly upon the side or gunwale of the canoe, with his feet in the inside of it, and then lifted him quite in, and set him close to his father, and presently stepping out again, launched the boat off, and paddled it along the shore faster than I could walk, though the wind blew pretty hard too. So he brought them both safe into our creek; and leaving them in the boat, runs away to fetch the other canoe. And as he passed me I spoke to him, and asked him whither he went? He told me, " Go fetch more boat." So away he went like the wind, for sure never man or horse run like him; and he had the other canoe in the creek almost as soon as I got to it by land. So he wafted me over, and then went to help our new guests out of the boat, which he did. But they were neither of them able to walk, so that poor Friday knew not what to do.

To remedy this I went to work in my thought, and calling to Friday to bid them sit down on the bank while he came to me, I soon made a kind of hand-barrow to lay them on, and Friday and I carried them up both together upon it between us. But when we got them to the outside of our wall or fortification we were at a worse loss than before, for it was impossible to get them over; and I was resolved not to break it down. So I set to work again; and Friday and I, in about two hours' time, made a very hand-some tent, covered with old sails, and above that with boughs of trees, being in the space without our outward fence, and between that and the grove of young wood which I had planted. And here we made them two beds of such things as I had, namely, of good rice-straw, with blankets laid upon it to lie on, and another to cover them on each bed.

My island was now peopled, and I thought myself very rich in subjects. And it was a merry reflection which I frequently made, how like a king I looked. First of all, the whole country was my own mere property, so that I had an undoubted right of domin-ion. Secondly, my people were perfectly subjected; I was absolute lord and lawgiver; they all owed their lives to me, and were ready to lay down their lives,

if there had been occasion of it, for me. It was remarkable, too, we had but three subjects and they
were of three different religions. My man Friday
was a Protestant, his father was a Pagan and a canni-
bal, and the Spaniard was a Papist.

However, I allowed liberty of conscience through-
out my dominions. But this is by the way.

As soon as I had secured my two weak rescued
prisoners, and given them shelter and a place to rest
them upon, I began to think of making some provision for them. And the first thing I did, I ordered
Friday to take a yearling goat—betwixt a kid and a
goat—out of my particular flock, to be killed, when
I cut off the hinder quarter, and chopping it into
small pieces, I set Friday to work to boiling and
stewing, and made them a very good dish, I assure
you, of flesh and broth, having put some barley and
rice also into the broth; and as I cooked it without
doors, for I made no fire within my inner wall, so I
carried it all into the new tent; and having set a table
there for them, I sat down and eat my own dinner
also with them, and, as well as I could, cheered them
and encouraged them; Friday being my interpreter,
especially to his father, and indeed to the Spaniard
too, for the Spaniard spoke the language of the savages pretty well.

Having now society enough, and our number being sufficient to put us out of fear of the savages if

they had come, unless their number had been very great, we went freely all over the island wherever we found occasion; and as here we had our escape or deliverance upon our thoughts, it was impossible, at least for me, to have the means of it out of mine. To this purpose I marked out several trees which I thought fit for our work, and I set Friday and his father to cutting them down; and then I caused the Spaniard, to whom I imparted my thought on that affair, to oversee and direct their work. I showed them with what indefatigable pains I had hewed a large tree into single planks, and I caused them to do the like till they had made about a dozen large planks of good oak, near two foot broad, thirty-five foot long, and from two inches to four inches thick. What prodigious labour it took up, anyone may imagine.

At the same time I contrived to increase my little flock of tame goats as much as I could, and to this purpose I made Friday and the Spaniard go out one day, and myself with Friday the next day; for we took our turns: and by this means we got above twenty young kids to breed up with the rest; for whenever we shot the dam, we saved the kids, and added them to our flock. But above all, the season for curing the grapes coming on, I caused such a prodigious quantity to be hung up in the sun, that I believe had we been at Alicant, where the raisins of the sun are cured, we could have filled sixty or eighty barrels. And these with our bread was a great part of our food; and very good living too, I assure you, for it is an exceeding nourishing food.

It was now harvest, and our crop in good order. It was not the most plentiful increase I had seen in the island, but however it was enough to answer our end; for from our twenty-two bushels of barley we brought in and thrashed out above two hundred and twenty bushels, and the like in proportion of the rice; which was store enough for our food to the next harvest, though all the sixteen Spaniards had been on shore with me; or if we had been ready for a voyage it would very plentifully have victualled our ship to have carried us to any part of the world—that is to say, of America.

When we had thus housed and secured our magazine of corn, we fell to work to make more wicker-work, namely, great baskets in which we kept it; and the Spaniard was very handy and dexterous at this part, and often blamed me that I did not make some things for defence of this kind of work; but I saw no need of it.

And now having a full supply of food for all the guests I expected, I gave the Spaniard leave to go over to the main to see what he could do with those he had left behind him there. I gave him a strict charge in writing not to bring any man with him who would not first swear in the presence of himself and of the old savage, that he would no way injure, fight with, or attack the person he should find in the island, who was so kind to send for them in order to their deliverance.

Under these instructions, the Spaniard and the old savage, the father of Friday, went away in one of the canoes which they might be said to come in, or rather were brought in, when they came as prisoners to be devoured by the savages. I gave each of them a musket with a firelock on it, and about eight charges of powder and ball, charging them to be very good husbands of both, and not to use either of them but upon urgent occasion. This was a cheerful work, being the first measures used by me in view of my deliverance for now twenty-seven years and some days. I gave them provisions of bread and of dried grapes sufficient for themselves for many days, and sufficient for all their countrymen for about eighty days' time; and wishing them a good voyage, I see them go, agreeing with them about a signal they should hang out at their return, by which I should know them again when they came back at a distance, before they came on shore.

They went away with a fair gale on the day that the moon was at full by my account, in the month of October. But as for an exact reckoning of days, after I had once lost it, I could never recover it again; nor had I kept even the number of years so punctually as to be sure that I was right, though, as it proved when I afterwards examined my account, I found I had kept a true reckoning of years.

It was no less than eight days I waited for them, when a strange and unforeseen accident intervened, of which the like has not perhaps been heard of in history. I was fast asleep in my hutch one morning, when my man Friday came running in to me and called aloud: " Master, master, they are come, they are come! " I jumped up, and regardless of danger, I went out as soon as I could get my clothes on, through my little grove, which, by the way, was by this time grown to be a very thick wood, I say, regardless of danger, I went without my arms, which was not my custom to do; but I was surprised when, turning my eyes to the sea, I presently saw a boat at about a league and half's distance, standing in for the shore with a shoulder-of-mutton sail, as they call it.

I had scarce set my foot on the hill when my eye plainly discovered a ship lying at an anchor, at about two leagues and a half's distance from me south-south-east, but not above a league and a half from the shore. By my observation it appeared plainly to be an English ship, and the boat appeared to be an English long-boat.

I cannot express the confusion I was in, though the joy of seeing a ship, and one who I had reason to believe was manned by my own countrymen and consequently friends, was such as I cannot describe. But yet I had some secret doubts hung about me, I cannot tell from whence they came, bidding me keep upon my guard. In the first place, it occurred to me to consider what business an English ship could have in that part of the world, since it was not the way to or from any part of the world where the English had any traffic; and I knew there had been no storms to drive them in there as in distress; and that if they were English really, it was most probable that they were here upon no good design, and that I had better continue as I was than fall into the hands of thieves and murderers.

I had not kept myself long in this posture, but I saw the boat draw near the shore, as if they looked for a creek to thrust in at for the convenience of landing. However, as they did not come quite far enough, they did not see the little inlet where I formerly landed my rafts, but run their boat on shore upon the beach, at about half a mile from me; which was very happy for me, for otherwise they would have landed just, as I may say, at my door, and would soon have beaten me out of my castle, and perhaps have plundered me of all I had.

When they were on shore I was fully satisfied that they were Englishmen, at least most of them. One or two I thought were Dutch; but it did not prove so. They were in all eleven men, whereof three of them

I found were unarmed, and, as I thought, bound; and when the first four or five of them were jumped on shore they took these three out of the boat as prisoners. One of the three I could perceive using the most passionate gestures of entreaty, affliction, and despair, even to a kind of extravagance; the other two, I could perceive, lifted up their hands sometimes, and appeared concerned indeed, but not to such a degree as the first.

I was perfectly confounded at the sight, and knew not what the meaning of it should be. Friday called out to me in English as well as he could: "O master! you see English mans eat prisoner as well as savage mans."—"Why," says I, "Friday, do you think they are a-going to eat them, then?"—"Yes," says Friday, "they will eat them."—"No, no," says I, "Friday; I am afraid they will murder them, indeed, but you may be sure they will not eat them."

All this while I had no thought of what the matter really was, but stood trembling with the horror of the sight, expecting every moment when the three prisoners should be killed; nay, once I saw one of the villains lift up his arm with a great cutlass, as the seamen call it, or sword, to strike one of the poor men; and I expected to see him fall every moment, at which all the blood in my body seemed to run chill in my veins.

After I had observed the outrageous usage of the

three men by the insolent seamen, I observed the fellows run scattering about the land as if they wanted to see the country. I observed that the three other men had liberty to go also where they pleased; but they sat down all three upon the ground, very pensive, and looked like men in despair. This put me in mind of the first time when I came on shore and began to look about me; how I gave myself over for lost; how wildly I looked round me; what dreadful apprehensions I had; and how I lodged in the tree all night for fear of being devoured by wild beasts.

As I knew nothing that night of the supply I was to receive by the providential driving of the ship nearer the land by the storms and tide, by which I have since been so long nourished and supported; so these three poor desolate men knew nothing how certain of deliverance and supply they were, how near it was to them, and how effectually and really they were in a condition of safety, at the same time that they thought themselves lost and their case desperate.

It was just at the top of high-water when these people came on shore, and while partly they stood parleying with the prisoners they brought, and partly while they rambled about to see what kind of a place they were in, they had carelessly stayed till the tide was spent and the water was ebbed considerably away, leaving their boat aground. They had left two men in the boat, who, as I found afterwards, having drank a little too much brandy, fell asleep; however, one of them waking sooner than the other, and finding the boat too fast aground for him to stir it, hallooed for the rest who were straggling about, upon which they all soon came to the boat; but it was past all their strength to launch her, the boat being very heavy, and the shore on that side being a soft oozy sand, almost like a quicksand.

In this condition, like true seamen, who are perhaps the least of all mankind given to forethought, they gave it over, and away they strolled about the country again; and I heard one of them say aloud to another, calling them off from the boat: "Why, let her alone, Jack, can't ye; she will float next tide;"— by which I was fully confirmed in the main inquiry of what countrymen they were.

All this while I kept myself very close, not once daring to stir out of my castle any farther than to my place of observation near the top of the hill; and very glad I was to think how well it was fortified. I knew it was no less than ten hours before the boat could be on float again, and by that time it would be dark, and I might be at more liberty to see their motions and to hear their discourse, if they had any.

In the meantime I fitted myself up for a battle as before; though with more caution, knowing I had to do with another kind of enemy than I had at first. I ordered Friday also, who I had made an excellent marksman with his gun, to load himself with arms. I took myself two fowling-pieces, and I gave him three muskets. My figure indeed was very fierce: I had my formidable goat-skin coat on, with the great cap I have mentioned, a naked sword by my side, two pistols in my belt, and a gun upon each shoulder. It was my design, as I said above, not to have made any attempt till it was dark; but about two o'clock, being the heat of the day, I found that in short they were all gone straggling into the woods, and, as I thought, were laid down to sleep. The three poor distressed men, too anxious for their condition to get any sleep, were, however, set down under the shelter of a great tree, at about a quarter of a mile from me, and, as I thought, out of sight of any of the rest. Upon this I resolved to discover myself to them, and learn something of their condition. Immediately I marched in the figure as above, my man Friday at a good distance behind me, as formidable for his arms as I, but not making quite so staring a spectre-like figure as I did.

I came as near them undiscovered as I could, and then, before any of them saw me, I called aloud to them in Spanish, "What are ye, gentlemen?"

They started up at the noise, but were ten times more confounded when they saw me, and the un-couth figure that I made. They made no answer at all, but I thought I perceived them just going to fly from me, when I spoke to them in English. "Gentlemen," said I, "do not be surprised at me; perhaps you may have a friend near you when you did not expect it."—"He must be sent directly from heaven then," said one of them very gravely to me, and pulling off his hat at the same time to me, "for our condition is past the help of man."—"All help is from heaven, sir," said I; "but can you put a stranger in the way how to help you, for you seem to me to be in some great distress? I saw you when you landed; and when you seemed to make applications to the brutes that came with you, I saw one of them lift up his sword to kill you."

The poor man, with tears running down his face, and trembling, looking like one astonished, returned, "Am I talking to God or man? Is it a real man or an angel?"—"Be in no fear about that, sir," said I; "if God had sent an angel to relieve you, he would have come better clothed, and armed after another manner than you see me in. Pray lay aside your fears; I am a man, an Englishman, and disposed to assist you, you see. I have one servant only; we have arms and ammunition; tell us freely. Can we serve you? What is your case?"

"Our case," said he, "sir, is too long to tell you while our murderers are so near; but in short, sir, I was commander of that ship; my men have mutinied against me; they have been hardly prevailed on not to murder me, and at last have set me on shore in this desolate place with these two men with me; one my mate, the other a passenger, where we expected to perish, believing the place to be uninhabited, and know not yet what to think of it."

"Where are those brutes, your enemies?" said I; "do you know where they are gone?"—"There they lie, sir," said he, pointing to a thicket of trees. "My heart trembles for fear they have seen us and heard you speak; if they have, they will certainly murder us all."

"Have they any firearms?" said I. He answered they had only two pieces, and one which they left in the boat. "Well then," said I, "leave the rest to me; I see they are all asleep; it is an easy thing to kill them all; but shall we rather take them prisoners?" He told me there were two desperate villains among them that it was scarce safe to show any mercy to; but if they were secured, he believed all the rest would return to their duty. I asked him which they were. He told me he could not at that distance describe them; but he would obey my orders in anything I would direct. "Well," says I, "let us retreat out of their view or hearing, lest they awake, and we will resolve further;" so they willingly went back with me till the woods covered us from them.

"Look you, sir," said I, "if I venture upon your deliverance, are you willing to make two conditions with me?" He anticipated my proposals by telling me that both he and the ship, if recovered, should be wholly directed and commanded by me in everything; and if the ship was not recovered, he would live and die with me in what part of the world soever I would send him; and the two other men said the same.

"Well," says I, "my conditions are but two:

1. That while you stay on this island with me you will not pretend to any authority here; and if I put arms into your hands, you will upon all occasions give them up to me, and do no prejudice to me or mine upon this island, and in the meantime be governed by my orders.

"2. That if the ship is, or may be recovered, you will carry me and my man to England passage free."

He gave me all the assurances that the invention and faith of man could devise, that he would comply with these most reasonable demands, and besides would owe his life to me, and acknowledge it upon all occasions as long as he lived.

"Well, then," said I, "here are three muskets for you, with powder and ball; tell me next what you think is proper to be done." He showed all the testimony of his gratitude that he was able; but offered to be wholly guided by me. I told him I thought it was hard venturing anything; but the best method I could think of was to fire upon them at once as they lay; and if any was not killed at the first volley, and offered to submit, we might save them, and so put it wholly upon God's providence to direct the shot.

He said very modestly that he was loath to kill them if he could help it, but that those two were incorrigible villains, and had been the authors of all the mutiny in the ship, and if they escaped we should be undone still; for they would go on board and bring the whole ship's company, and destroy us all. "Well then," says I, "necessity legitimates my advice, for it is the only way to save our lives." However, seeing him still cautious of shedding blood, I told him they should go themselves, and manage as they found convenient.

In the middle of this discourse we heard some of them awake, and soon after we saw two of them on their feet. I asked him if either of them were of the men who he had said were the heads of the mutiny? He said, "No." "Well then," said I, "you may let them escape; and Providence seems to have wakened them on purpose to save themselves. Now," says I, "if the rest escape you, it is your fault."

Animated with this, he took the musket I had given him in his hand, and a pistol in his belt, and his two comrades with him, with each man a piece in his hand. The two men who were with him, going first, made some noise, at which one of the seamen who was awake turned about, and seeing them coming, cried out to the rest. But it was too late then; for the moment he cried out, they fired—I mean the two men, the captain wisely reserving his own piece. They had so well aimed their shot at the men they knew, that one of them was killed on the spot, and the other very much wounded; but not being dead, he started up upon his feet, and called eagerly for help to the other; but the captain, stepping to him, told him it was too late to cry for help, he should call upon God to forgive his villainy, and with that word knocked him down with the stock of his musket, so that he never spoke more. There were three more in the company, and one of them was also slightly wounded. By this time I was come, and when they saw their danger, and that it was in vain to resist, they begged for mercy. The captain told them he would spare their lives if they would give him any assurance of their abhorrence of the treachery they had been guilty of, and would swear to be faithful to him in recovering the ship, and afterwards in carrying her back to Jamaica, from whence they came. They gave him all the protestations of their sincerity that could be desired, and he was willing to believe them and spare their lives, which I was not against; only I obliged him to keep them bound hand and foot while they were upon the island.

While this was doing, I sent Friday with the captain's mate to the boat, with orders to secure her and bring away the oars and sail; which they did. And by and by, three straggling men, that were (happily for them) parted from the rest, came back upon hearing the guns fired; and seeing their captain, who before was their prisoner, now their conqueror, they submitted to be bound also, and so our victory was complete.

It now remained that the captain and I should inquire into one another's circumstances. I began first, and told him my whole history, which he heard with an attention even to amazement; and particularly at the wonderful manner of my being furnished with provisions and ammunition. And, indeed, as my story is a whole collection of wonders, it affected him deeply.

After this communication was at end I carried him and his two men into my apartment, leading them in just where I came out, namely, at the top of the house, where I refreshed them with such provisions as I had, and showed them all the contrivances I had made during my long, long inhabiting that place.

All I showed them, all I said to them, was perfectly amazing; but above all, the captain admired my fortification, and how perfectly I had concealed my retreat with a grove of trees, which, having been now planted near twenty years, and the trees growing much faster than in England, was become a little wood, and so thick that it was unpassable in any part of it but at that one side where I had reserved my little winding passage into it. I told him this was my castle and my residence, but that I had a seat in the country, as most princes have, whither I could retreat upon occasion, and I would show him that too another time, but at present our business was to consider how to recover the ship. He agreed with me as to that, but told me he was perfectly at a loss what measures to take; for that there were still six-and-twenty hands on board, who, having entered into a cursed conspiracy, by which they had all forfeited their lives to the law, would be hardened in it now by desperation, and would carry it on, knowing that if they were reduced they should be brought to the gallows.

I mused for some time upon what he had said, and found it was a very rational conclusion, and that therefore something was to be resolved on very speedily, as well to draw the men on board into some snare for their surprise as to prevent their landing upon us and destroying us. Upon this it presently occurred to me that in a little while the ship's crew, wondering what was become of their comrades and of the boat, would certainly come on shore in their other boat to seek for them, and that then perhaps they might come armed, and be too strong for us. This he allowed was rational.

Upon this I told him the first thing we had to do

was to stave the boat which lay upon the beach, so
that they might not carry her off; and taking everything out of her, leave her so far useless as not to be
fit to swim. Accordingly we went on board, took the
arms which were left on board out of her, and whatever else we found there, which was a bottle of
brandy and another of rum, a few biscuit cakes, a
horn of powder, and a great lump of sugar in a piece
of canvas—the sugar was five or six pounds; all
which was very welcome to me, especially the brandy
and sugar, of which I had had none left for many
years. When we had carried all these things on shore
(the oars, mast, sail, and rudder of the boat were
carried away before, as above), we knocked a great
hole in her bottom.

While we were thus preparing our designs, and
had first by main strength heaved the boat up upon
the beach so high that the tide would not float her
off at high-water mark; and besides, had broke a
hole in her bottom too big to be quickly stopped,
and were sat down musing what we should do; we
heard the ship fire a gun, and saw her make a waft
with her ancient, as a signal for the boat to come on
board; but no boat stirred; and they fired several
times, making other signals for the boat.

At last, when all their signals and firings proved
fruitless, and they found the boat did not stir, we
saw them by the help of my glasses hoist another

boat out and row towards the shore, and we found as they approached that there was no less than ten men in her, and that they had firearms with them. As the ship lay almost two leagues from the shore, we had a full view of them as they came, and a plain sight of the men, even of their faces; because the tide having set them a little to the east of the other boat, they rowed up under shore to come to the same place where the other had landed, and where the boat lay. By this means, I say, we had a full view of them, and the captain knew the persons and characters of all the men in the boat, of whom he said that there were three very honest fellows, who, he was sure, were led into this conspiracy by the rest, being over-powered and frighted. But that as for the boatswain, who it seems was the chief officer among them, and all the rest, they were as outrageous as any of the ship's crew, and were no doubt made desperate in their new enterprise; and terribly apprehensive he was that they would be too powerful for us.

I smiled at him, and told him that men in our circumstances were past the operation of fear: that seeing almost every condition that could be was better than that which we were supposed to be in, we ought to expect that the consequence, whether death or life, would be sure to be a deliverance. I asked him what he thought of the circumstances of my life, and whether a deliverance were not worth venturing for?

"And where, sir," said I, "is your belief of my being preserved here on purpose to save your life, which elevated you a little while ago? For my part," said I, "there seems to be but one thing amiss in all the prospect of it." "What's that?" says he. "Why," said I, "'tis that, as you say, there are three or four honest fellows among them, which should be spared. Had they been all of the wicked part of the crew, I should have thought God's providence had singled them out to deliver them into your hands; for, depend upon it, every man of them that comes ashore are our own, and shall die or live as they behave to us."

As I spoke this with a raised voice and cheerful countenance, I found it greatly encouraged him; so we set vigorously to our business. We had upon the first appearance of the boat's coming from the ship considered of separating our prisoners, and had indeed secured them effectually.

Two of them, of whom the captain was less assured than ordinary, I sent with Friday, and one of the three (delivered men) to my cave, where they were remote enough, and out of danger of being heard or discovered, or of finding their way out of the woods if they could have delivered themselves. Here they left them bound, but gave them provisions.

The other prisoners had better usage. Two of them were kept pinioned indeed, because the captain was not free to trust them, but the other two were taken into my service upon their captain's recommendation, and upon their solemnly engaging to live and die with us. So with them and the three honest men, we were seven men, well armed; and I made no doubt we should be able to deal well enough with the ten that were a-coming, considering that the captain had said there were three or four honest men among them also.

As soon as they got to the place where their other boat lay, they run their boat into the beach, and came all on shore, hauling the boat up after them. Being on shore, the first thing they did, they ran all to their other boat; and it was easy to see that they were under a great surprise to find her stripped, as above, of all that was in her, and a great hole in her bottom. After they had mused a while upon this, they set up two or three great shouts, hallooing with all their might, to try if they could make their companions hear; but all was to no purpose. Then they came all close in a ring, and fired a volley of their small arms; which indeed we heard, and the echoes made the woods ring, but it was all one; those in the cave, we were sure, could not hear; and those in our keeping, though they heard it well enough, yet durst give no answer to them. They were so astonished at the surprise of this, that they immediately launched their boat again, and got all of them on board.

They had not been long put off with the boat, but

we perceived them all coming on shore again; but with this new measure in their conduct, which it seems they consulted together upon—namely, to leave three men in the boat, and the rest to go on shore, and go up into the country to look for their fellows.

This was a great disappointment to us, for now we were at a loss what to do; for our seizing those seven men on shore would be no advantage to us if we let the boat escape; because they would then row away to the ship, and then the rest of them would be sure to weigh and set sail, and so our recovering the ship would be lost. However, we had no remedy but to wait and see what the issue of things might present. The seven men came on shore, and the three who remained in the boat put her off to a good distance from the shore, and came to an anchor to wait for them; so that it was impossible for us to come at them in the boat.

Those that came on shore kept close together, marching towards the top of the little hill under which my habitation lay; and we could see them plainly, though they could not perceive us. But when they were come to the brow of the hill, where they could see a great way into the valleys and woods which lay towards the north-east part, and where the island lay lowest, they shouted and hallooed till they were weary; and not caring, it seems, to venture far from the shore, nor far from one another, they sat down together under a tree to consider of it. We waited a great while, though very impatient for their removing; and were very uneasy when, after long consultations, we saw them start all up and march down towards the sea. As soon as I perceived them go towards the shore I presently thought of a stratagem to fetch them back again, and which answered my end to a tittle. I ordered Friday and the captain's mate to go over the little creek westward, towards the place where the savages came on shore when Friday was rescued; and as soon as they came to a little rising ground at about half a mile distance I bade them halloo as loud as they could, and wait till they found the seamen heard them; that as soon as ever they heard the seamen answer them they should return it again; and then, keeping out of sight, take a round, always answering when the other hallooed, to draw them as far into the island, and among the woods, as possible; and then wheel about again to me by such ways as I directed them.

They were just going into the boat when Friday and the mate hallooed; and they presently heard them, and answering, run along the shore westward, towards the voice they heard, when they were presently stopped by the creek, where the water being up, they could not get over, and called for the boat to come up and set them over, as indeed I expected.

When they had set themselves over, I observed that the boat being gone up a good way into the creek, and, as it were, in a harbour within the land, they took one of the three men out of her to go along with them, and left only two in the boat, having fastened her to the stump of a little tree on the shore.

This was what I wished for, and immediately leaving Friday and the captain's mate to their business, I took the rest with me, and crossing the creek out of their sight, we surprised the two men before they were aware; one of them lying on shore, and the other being in the boat. The fellow on shore was between sleeping and waking, and going to start up, the captain, who was foremost, ran in upon him and knocked him down, and then called out to him in the boat to yield, or he was a dead man.

There needed very few arguments to persuade a single man to yield when he saw five men upon him, and his comrade knocked down; besides, this was, it seems, one of the three who were not so hearty in the mutiny as the rest of the crew, and therefore was easily persuaded not only to yield, but afterwards to join very sincerely with us.

In the meantime Friday and the captain's mate so well managed their business with the rest, that they drew them, by hallooing and answering, from one hill to another, and from one wood to another, till they not only heartily tired them, but left them where they were

very sure they could not reach back to the boat before it was dark; and indeed they were heartily tired
themselves also by the time they came back to us.

We had nothing now to do but to watch for them
in the dark, and to fall upon them, so as to make
sure work with them.

It was several hours after Friday came back to me
before they came back to their boat: and we could
hear the foremost of them long before they came
quite up, calling to those behind to come along; and
could also hear them answer and complain how lame
and tired they were, and not able to come any faster—
which was very welcome news to us.

At length they came up to the boat; but 'tis impossible to express their confusion when they found the
boat fast aground in the creek, the tide ebbed out,
and their two men gone! We could hear them call to
one another in a most lamentable manner, telling
one another they were gotten into an enchanted island: that either there were inhabitants in it, and they
should all be murdered, or else there were devils and
spirits in it, and they should be all carried away and
devoured.

They hallooed again, and called their two comrades by their names a great many times; but no
answer. After some time we could see them, by the
little light there was, run about wringing their hands
like men in despair; and that sometimes they would

go and sit down in the boat to rest themselves, then come ashore again and walk about again, and so the same thing over again.

My men would fain have me give them leave to fall upon them at once in the dark; but I was willing to take them at some advantage so to spare them, and kill as few of them as I could; and especially I was unwilling to hazard the killing any of our own men, knowing the other were very well armed. I resolved to wait to see if they did not separate; and therefore to make sure of them I drew my ambuscade nearer, and ordered Friday and the captain to creep upon their hands and feet as close to the ground as they could, that they might not be discovered, and get as near them as they could possibly, before they offered to fire.

They had not been long in that posture but that the boatswain, who was the principal ringleader of the mutiny, and had now shown himself the most dejected and dispirited of all the rest, came walking towards them with two more of their crew. The captain was so eager, as having this principal rogue so much in his power, that he could hardly have patience to let him come so near as to be sure of him; for they only heard his tongue before. But when they came nearer, the captain and Friday, starting up on their feet, let fly at them.

The boatswain was killed upon the spot, the next

man was shot into the body, and fell just by him, though he did not die till an hour or two after; and the third ran for it.

At the noise of the fire I immediately advanced with my whole army, which was now eight men namely, myself *generalissimo*, Friday my lieutenant-general, the captain and his two men, and the three prisoners of war, who we had trusted with arms.

We came upon them indeed in the dark, so that they could not see our number; and I made the man we had left in the boat, who was now one of us call to them by name, to try if I could bring them to a parley, and so might perhaps reduce them to terms. So he calls out as loud as he could to one of them, "Tom Smith! Tom Smith!" Tom Smith answered immediately, "Who's that, Robinson?" for it seems he knew his voice. The other answered "Ay, ay; for God's sake, Tom Smith, throw down your arms and yield, or you are all dead men this moment."

"Who must we yield to? where are they?" says Smith again. "Here they are," says he; "here's our captain, and fifty men with him, have been hunting you this two hours. The boatswain is killed, Will Frye is wounded, and I am a prisoner; and if you do not yield, you are all lost."

"Will they give us quarter, then," says Tom Smith, "and we will yield?" "I'll go and ask, if you promise to yield," says Robinson. So he asked the captain, and the captain then calls himself out, "You, Smith, you know my voice, if you lay down your arms immediately and submit, you shall have your lives— all but Will Atkins."

Upon this Will Atkins cried out, "For God's sake, captain, give me quarter! What have I done? They have been all as bad as I;" which, by the way, was not true neither; for it seems this Will Atkins was the first man that laid hold of the captain when they first mutinied, and used him barbarously, in tying his hands and giving him injurious language. However, the captain told him he must lay down his arms at discretion, and trust to the governor's mercy; by which he meant me, for they all called me governor.

In a word, they all laid down their arms, and begged their lives; and I sent the man that had parleyed with them, and two more, who bound them all; and then my great army of fifty men, which particularly with those three, were all but eight, came up and seized upon them all, and upon their boat—only that I kept myself and one more out of sight, for reasons of state.

They all appeared very penitent, and begged hard for their lives. As for that, the captain told them, they were none of his prisoners, but the commander of the island; that they thought they had set him on shore in a barren, uninhabited island, but it had pleased God so to direct them, that the island was inhabited, and that the governor was an Englishman that he might hang them all there if he pleased; but as he had given them all quarter, he supposed he would send them to England to be dealt with there as justice required—except Atkins, who he was commanded by the governor to advise to prepare for death, for that he would be hanged in the morning.

Though this was all a fiction of his own, yet it had its desired effect. Atkins fell upon his knees to beg the captain to intercede with the governor for his life, and all the rest begged of him for God's sake that they might not be sent to England.

It now occurred to me that the time of our deliverance was come, and that it would be a most easy thing to bring these fellows in to be hearty in getting possession of the ship; so I retired in the dark from them, that they might not see what kind of a governor they had, and called the captain to me. When I called, as at a good distance, one of the men was ordered to speak again, and say to the captain, "Captain, the commander calls for you." And presently the captain replied, "Tell his excellency I am just a-coming." This more perfectly amused them; and they all believed that the commander was just by with his fifty men.

Upon the captain's coming to me I told him my project for seizing the ship, which he liked of wonderfully well, and resolved to put it in execution the next morning.

But in order to execute it with more art, and secure

of success, I told him we must divide the prisoners, and that he should go and take Atkins and two more of the worst of them, and send them pinioned to the cave where the others lay. This was committed to Friday and the two men who came on shore with the captain.

They conveyed them to the cave as to a prison; and it was indeed a dismal place, especially to men in their condition.

The others I ordered to my bower, as I called it, of which I have given a full description; and as it was fenced in, and they pinioned, the place was secure enough, considering they were upon their behaviour.

To these in the morning I sent the captain, who was to enter into a parley with them; in a word, to try them, and tell me whether he thought they might be trusted or no to go on board and surprise the ship. He talked to them of the injury done him, of the condition they were brought to, and that though the governor had given them quarter for their lives as to the present action, yet that if they were sent to England they would all be hanged in chains, to be sure; but that if they would join in so just an attempt as to recover the ship, he would have the governor's engagement for their pardon.

Anyone may guess how readily such a proposal would be accepted by men in their condition. They fell down on their knees to the captain, and promised, with the deepest imprecations, that they would be faithful to him to the last drop, and that they should owe their lives to him, and would go with him all over the world; that they would own him for a father to them as long as they lived.

"Well," says the captain, "I must go and tell the governor what you say, and see what I can do to bring him to consent to it." So he brought me an account of the temper he found them in, and that he verily believed they would be faithful.

However, that we might be very secure, I told him he should go back again, and choose out five of them, and tell them they might see that he did not want men, that he would take out those five to be his assistants, and that the governor would keep the other two, and the three that were sent prisoners to the castle (my cave) as hostages, for the fidelity of those five; and that if they proved unfaithful in the execution, the five hostages should be hanged in chains alive upon the shore.

This looked severe, and convinced them that the governor was in earnest. However, they had no way left them but to accept it, and it was now the business of the prisoners, as much as of the captain, to persuade the other five to do their duty.

Our strength was now thus ordered for the expedition: 1. The captain, his mate, and passenger; 2. Then the two prisoners of the first gang, to whom, having their characters from the captain, I had given their liberty, and trusted them with arms; 3. The other two who I had kept till now in my bower pinioned, but upon the captain's motion had now released; 4. These five released at last: so that they were twelve in all, besides five we kept prisoners in the cave for hostages.

I asked the captain if he was willing to venture with these hands on board the ship; for as for me and my man Friday, I did not think it was proper for us to stir, having seven men left behind, and it was employment enough for us to keep them asunder and supply them with victuals.

When I showed myself to the two hostages, it was with the captain, who told them I was the person the governor had ordered to look after them, and that it was the governor's pleasure they should not stir anywhere but by my direction; that if they did, they should be fetched into the castle and be laid in irons. So that as we never suffered them to see me as governor, so I now appeared as another person, and spoke of the governor, the garrison, the castle, and the like, upon all occasions.

The captain now had no difficulty before him but to furnish his two boats, stop the breach of one, and man them. And they contrived their business very well, for they came up to the ship about midnight. As soon as they came within call of the ship he made Robinson hail them, and tell them they had brought off the men and the boat, but that it was a long time before they had found them, and the like, holding them in a chat till they came to the ship's side; when the captain and the mate, entering first with their arms, immediately knocked down the second mate and carpenter with the butt-end of their muskets. Being very faithfully seconded by their men, they secured all the rest that were upon the main and quarter-decks, and began to fasten the hatches to keep them down who were below, when the other boat and their men, entering at the fore-chains, secured the forecastle of the ship, and the scuttle which went down into the cook-room, making three men they found there prisoners.

When this was done, and all safe upon deck, the captain ordered the mate with three men to break into the round-house,* where the new rebel captain lay, and having taken the alarm, was gotten up, and with two men and a boy had gotten firearms in their hands; and when the mate with a crow split open the door, the new captain and his men fired boldly among them, and wounded the mate with a musket-ball, which broke his arm, and wounded two more of the men, but killed nobody.

The mate, calling for help, rushed, however, into

---

* At that time, the upper cabin in the stern of the ship was the master's room, and was called the round-house, probably because it had a round top raised above the deck.

the round-house, wounded as he was, and with his pistol shot the new captain through the head; upon which the rest yielded, and the ship was taken effectually, without any more lives lost.

As soon as the ship was thus secured, the captain ordered seven guns to be fired, which was the signal agreed upon with me to give me notice of his success; which, you may be sure, I was very glad to hear, having sat watching upon the shore for it till near two of the clock in the morning.

Having thus heard the signal plainly, I laid me down; and it having been a day of great fatigue to me, I slept very sound, till I was something surprised with the noise of a gun; and presently starting up, I heard a man call me by the name of " Governor, governor;" and presently I knew the captain's voice, when climbing up to the top of the hill, there he stood, and pointing to the ship he embraced me in his arms. " My dear friend and deliverer," says he, "there's your ship; for she is all yours, and so are we and all that belong to her." I cast my eyes to the ship, and there she rode within little more than half a mile of the shore.

I was at first ready to sink down with the surprise; for I saw my deliverance indeed visibly put into my hands, all things easy, and a large ship just ready to carry me away whither I pleased to go. At first, for some time, I was not able to answer him one word but as he had taken me in his arms I held fast by him, or I should have fallen to the ground.

When he had talked a while the captain told me he had brought me some little refreshment, such as the ship afforded, and such as the wretches that had been so long his masters had not plundered him of. Upon this, he called aloud to the boat, and bid his men bring the things ashore that were for the governor.

After these ceremonies past, and after all his good things were brought into my little apartment, we began to consult what was to be done with the prisoners we had; for it was worth considering whether we might venture to take them away with us or no, especially two of them, who we knew to be incorrigible and refractory to the last degree; and the captain said he knew they were such rogues that there was no obliging them, and if he did carry them away it must be in irons as malefactors to be delivered over to justice at the first English colony he could come at. And I found that the captain himself was very anxious about it.

Upon this, I told him that if he desired it I durst undertake to bring the two men he spoke of to make it their own request that he should leave them upon the island. "I should be very glad of that," says the captain, "with all my heart."

"Well," says I, "I will send for them up, and talk with them for you." So I caused Friday and the two hostages—for they were now discharged, their comrades having performed their promise; I say, I caused them to go to the cave and bring up the five men, pinioned as they were, to the bower, and keep them there till I came.

After some time I came thither dressed in my new habit, and now I was called governor again. Being all met, and the captain with me, I caused the men to be brought before me, and I told them I had had a full account of their villainous behaviour to the captain, and how they had run away with the ship, and were preparing to commit farther robberies, but that Providence had ensnared them in their own ways, and that they were fallen into the pit which they had digged for others.

I let them know that by my direction the ship had been seized, that she lay now in the road, and they might see by and by that their new captain had received the reward of his villainy, for that they might see him hanging at the yard-arm.

That as to them, I wanted to know what they had to say why I should not execute them as pirates taken in the fact, as by my commission they could not doubt I had authority to do.

One of them answered, in the name of the rest, that they had nothing to say but this, that when they were taken the captain promised them their lives; and they humbly implored my mercy. But I told them I knew not what mercy to show them; for as for myself I had resolved to quit the island with all my men, and had taken passage with the captain to go for England, and as for the captain he could not carry them to England other than as prisoners in irons to be tried for mutiny and running away with the ship, the consequence of which, they must needs know, would be the gallows: so that I could not tell which was best for them, unless they had a mind to take their fate in the island. If they desired that (I did not care, as I had liberty to leave it), I had some inclination to give them their lives, if they thought they could shift on shore.

They seemed very thankful for it, said they would much rather venture to stay there than to be carried to England to be hanged. So I left it on that issue.

However, the captain seemed to make some difficulty of it, as if he durst not leave them there. Upon this I seemed a little angry with the captain, and told him that they were my prisoners, not his; and that seeing I had offered them so much favour, I would be as good as my word; and that if he did not think fit to consent to it, I would set them at liberty as I found them, and if he did not like it, he might take them again if he could catch them.

Upon this they appeared very thankful, and I accordingly set them at liberty, and bade them retire into the woods to the place whence they came, and I would leave them some firearms, some ammunition, and some directions how they should live very well if they thought fit.

I left them my firearms, namely, five muskets, three fowling-pieces, and three swords. I had above a barrel and a half of powder left; for after the first year or two I used but little and wasted none. I gave them a description of the way I managed the goats, and directions to milk and fatten them, and to make both butter and cheese.

In a word, I gave them every part of my own story. And I told them I would prevail with the captain to leave them two barrels of gunpowder more, and some garden-seeds, which I told them I would have been very glad of; also I gave them the bag of pease which the captain had brought me to eat, and bade them be sure to sow and increase them.

Having done all this I left them the next day, and went on board the ship. We prepared immediately to sail, but did not weigh that night. The next morning early two of the five men came swimming to the ship's side, and making a most lamentable complaint of the other three, begged to be taken into the ship, for God's sake, for they should be murdered and begged the captain to take them on board though he hanged them immediately.

Upon this the captain pretended to have no power without me. But after some difficulty, and after their solemn promises of amendment, they were taken on board, and were some time after soundly whipped and pickled;* after which they proved very honest and quiet fellows.

Some time after this the boat was ordered on shore, the tide being up, with the things promised to the men; to which the captain, at my intercession, caused their chests and clothes to be added; which they took, and were very thankful for. I also encouraged them by telling them that if it lay in my way to send any vessel to take them in, I would not forget them.

When I took leave of this island I carried on board for relics the great goat-skin cap I had made, my umbrella, and my parrot; also I forgot not to take the money I formerly mentioned, which had lain by me so long useless that it was grown rusty, or tarnished, and could hardly pass for silver till it had been a little rubbed and handled.

And thus I left the island the 19th of December, as I found by the ship's account, in the year 1686, after I had been upon it eight-and-twenty years, two months, and nineteen days. In this vessel, after a long voyage, I arrived in England the 11th of June, in the year 1687, having been thirty-and-five years absent.

* When sailors were flogged the punishment was sometimes increased by pouring salt water or brine upon the sore places made by the lash. This was called "pickling".